THE
BLOODROCK
VALLEY WAR

*Also by Ray Hogan
in Thorndike Large Print* ®

Hell Raiser
Solitude's Lawman

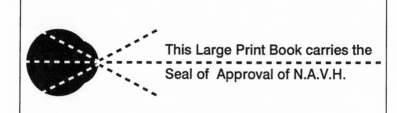

This Large Print Book carries the
Seal of Approval of N.A.V.H.

THE BLOODROCK VALLEY WAR

RAY HOGAN

Thorndike Press • Thorndike, Maine

Library of Congress Cataloging in Publication Data:

Hogan, Ray, 1908-
    The Bloodrock Valley war / Ray Hogan.
        p. cm.
    ISBN 1-56054-573-9 (alk. paper : lg. print)
    1. Large type books. I. Title.
[PS3558.O3473B57   1992]   92-35422
813'.54—dc20   CIP

Thorndike Large Print® Western Series edition published
in 1992 by arrangement with Donald MacCampbell, Inc.

Cover design by Bruce Habowksi, Jr.

This book is printed on acid-free, high opacity paper. ∞

THE BLOODROCK VALLEY WAR

I

"Here they come," Aaron Cash said, cradling his shotgun and stepping back into the shadows of the tamarisk windbreak.

Ben Keenlyn moved forward to the edge of the porch, touching the weapon in the hands of the hawk-faced old puncher with a sharp glance.

"Be no need for that," he said quietly.

Cash shrugged his bony shoulders. "Any time a man's dealing with a sidewinder like Pete Amber and that no-good whelp of his'n, he needs an ace in the hole. You just don't pay me no mind. Do your gabblin', I'll do the watching."

Ben swung his attention to the twin ruts leading up to his place from the road that bisected Bloodrock Valley. Six riders in the party. They were still at considerable distance, but he recognized each easily. They weren't going to like what he had to tell them.

Pete Amber was in the lead, a big, white-haired, hard-faced man. Pete rode a horse as if he were king and everyone else his subjects. Felt that way about it too.

To his left was his son, Jack, growing up in his father's shadow — and image. At twenty-five, only a year younger than Ben, Jack was every bit as autocratic and ruthless as his parent.

To the elder Amber's right was Gorman Hensley, the land agent. His home was in Denver, but he was quartering at Moriarity's Hotel in nearby Ute Springs while he negotiated the purchase of the valley. Hensley's clients were a half dozen moneyed men who wished to get into the cattle business on a large scale. Their plan was to consolidate the five ranches in the valley into one.

The fourth man was Ed Suber, who had inherited the E Bar S when his father died. Ed was no rancher; he was interested mostly in gambling and drinking and having his time with the saloon girls. He was anxious to accept Gorman Hensley's offer and sell out.

On one side of Suber was old Fritz Kemmer, whose Double Diamond outfit lay due north of Amber's vast Seven Bar. Red faced, snowy haired, and well up in his sixties, Kemmer, too, was willing to sell. He was tired, he'd told Ben, wanted to quit. But that was a different story from what Keenlyn had heard earlier — before Kemmer's barn had burned to the ground.

The sixth man was Homer Ragland, whose niece Marcie, Ben hoped to marry. Ragland owned Arrowhead, north of and adjoining

Keenlyn's Box K which lay at the entrance to the valley. Homer's wife, Emerald, was the most beautiful woman Ben had ever seen — tall, exquisitely shaped, with black hair, creamy skin, and eyes green as spring fern.

Unfortunately, Emerald's striking beauty was no more than surface deep. Cold, austere, and with a tongue sharp as flint, it was as if some god with a flair for breathtaking loveliness had created her from flawless marble, added color, but failed completely to add warmth.

Emerald was at the bottom of Homer Ragland's desire to sell. Ben knew this from speaking with Marcie and listening to the rancher himself. She had no taste for being a rancher's wife. She wanted only to return to what she termed civilization, in Kansas City.

Keenlyn's glance traveled over the grass-covered flats and gentle slopes of the Box K. He'd been successful too, in a small way. He'd taken over after the death of his father from lung fever eight years back, and with Aaron Cash and old Casimiro Valdez, the Mexican cook, standing by him, he had everything in fairly good shape.

By careful handling he'd increased his herd to somewhere around fifteen hundred head, selling only enough each year to pay expenses and accomplish a few improvements.

Tom Keenlyn had been a wise man. He had been the first to settle in Bloodrock Valley, and although his place was not as large as the other spreads, it was by far the choicest land and the best situated.

It was the nearest to Ute Springs, the settlement upon which all depended for supplies, and had ample water from the Solano River and Bear Creek.

Further, the position of the Box K was ideal insofar as access to the railhead at Dalhart was concerned. He had but to drive his herds along Bear Creek, through a break in the Feather Mountains, and onto the broad plains beyond, at the far side of which was the shipping point.

Other ranchers in the valley were forced to use the northern trail, a long, difficult, almost waterless route that wound its way across the upper edge of Ragland's property. All but Pete Amber. Pete had come into the valley a year after Tom Keenlyn. They'd become friends, and they'd made a gentleman's agreement that Amber was to have trail rights across Box K range for as long as he wished.

Ben had always honored the handshake deal between his father and Pete Amber and would continue to do so despite his dislike for the man, his son, and Seven Bar in general. The arrangement, he knew, had become a thorn in Pete Amber's side as the years passed; it galled the despotic rancher to be dependent upon another. . . .

Hensley wanted the valley for his clients with no strings attached — all or nothing was the way he put it. Everyone had agreed to the sale except Ben, who wanted to think it over and had promised to give his answer at a later date. And now Pete Amber and the others were coming to hear that answer.

Keenlyn raised his glance to the riders filing into the yard, realizing suddenly that Gabe Carlin, who bore the title of Seven Bar foreman but whose duties seemed to consist mostly of siding Jack Amber wherever he went, was absent. Such was unusual; where you saw one you saw the other. Evidently Pete had ruled that only the ranchers and Gorman Hensley were to make the call.

Hooking his thumbs in his gunbelt, Ben stepped off the porch into the pale glare of the dying sun and waited in silence as the riders pulled up. Pete Amber brushed his broad-brimmed hat to the back of his head, thrust forward his hard-cornered face and squinted down at Keenlyn.

"Well," he demanded in a harsh, impatient voice. "What's it to be?"

"Answer's no," Ben said. "I'm not selling."

Pete stiffened, and an angry flush suffused

his features. Jack muttered something, and Homer Ragland sighed gustily. Ignoring them, Pete Amber leaned forward, pinned Ben with a hard glare.

"I ain't taking that for an answer," he said coldly. No two-bit cow nurse is going to mess up my deal . . . not now — not ever!"

II

Ben Keenlyn drew himself up stiffly as anger flashed through him. A tense hush fell during which the only sound was the nervous fidgeting of Pete Amber's stallion.

Hensley, calm and neat in his gray business suit, finally broke the silence. "Can't understand you, Keenlyn. Offered you a fair price — a good one, in fact. Figured you'd go for it."

Ben shrugged. "Told you the other night I wasn't much interested."

"Admit that, but you agreed to think it over —"

"I did. Decided I didn't want to sell."

"Makes you the only one in the valley holding out. And the town's for it too. Mean a lot to the merchants — new people moving in, new money."

"Hell with all that bullraw!" Pete Amber shouted abruptly. "We been all through it before!" Jerking off his hat, he shoved his leonine head forward, black eyes snapping.

"What's the reason, Keenlyn? You wanting more money for this — this cabbage patch?"

Ben could not suppress a smile. "Not that," he answered. "Fact is, I don't *want* to sell."

13

Ragland's tone was harried, desperate. "You're spoiling the deal for all of us. Reckon you know that."

"No need to," Ben said. "I'll give the same trail rights to Hensley's people that my pa gave to Seven Bar."

"No, I'm afraid that's not good enough," the land agent said. "Thought I made that clear the other night — and a handshake's not good business."

"Good as a lawyer's contract far as I'm concerned, but if it'll help, I'll put it in writing."

"They won't go for that either," Hensley said. "The deal's for every acre in the valley. Your place tucked down here in the corner would be like a gun pointed at their head."

"Only if they make it so," Ben said wearily, and stepped back up onto the porch. "Don't like being the one who queers the sale, but you've got my answer. Be no changing it."

"Maybe you ain't realizing how unpopular you're going to be around here with folks," Suber said. "And in this country a man needs friends."

"And he'll be needing plenty of them," Jack Amber said pointedly, "if he don't go along with us."

Ben shifted his gaze to the younger man. "If it's trouble you're planning, expect I can hold up my end."

The younger Amber laughed. "What with? That old crowbait you've had hanging around here for years and them three saddle tramps you call a crew? Hell, I can send my yard hands down here and —"

"Shut up, Jack," Pete said in a flat, dispassionate voice. "Howsomever, he's got a point there, Keenlyn," he added, again leaning forward and impaling Ben with his eyes. "You ain't got a chance, bucking us. The town, too. If nothing else we can starve you out."

"You're welcome to try. Can always haul my supplies in from Buford's Crossing or some other town. Doubt if that'll ever be necessary as long as Seligman's in business."

"Which maybe he won't be."

Keenlyn felt a twinge of concern. Sol Seligman, while seeing some advantage to the change in the valley, had nevertheless stood up for Ben and his right to refuse.

"Leave Sol out of this," Keenlyn said, his voice taut. "Anything happens to him or his place, I'll hold you accountable and take it to the U. S. Marshal."

"U. S. Marshal?" Jack mocked. "What's that?"

"Nothing's going to happen to him," Pete said. "Just trying to show you what you're up against — you and anybody who fancies being your friend."

"Expect Marcie's got some ideas about this, too," Ragland added. "You talk to her?"

Ben had, and Marcie, torn between her feeling for him and a loyalty to the uncle who had taken her in when her parents died, could be of no help.

"We've talked."

"And?"

"It's between us, nobody else," Ben said coolly. "Has nothing to do —"

"Has plenty to do with me!" Ragland countered in a wild sort of voice. "Being my niece, I got a right to know."

"Marcie's of age. Expect she'll make up her own mind," Keenlyn said, and dropped the subject. "Appreciate your offer," he added, directing his attention to Gorman Hensley. "I'm willing to grant you crossing rights, just as I said, but I won't sell."

The land agent lifted his hands, allowed them to fall as he glanced around at the men clustered about him.

"Well, gentlemen, that seems to be it. You know how my clients feel about it — all of the valley or none. Appears to be none. I'll notify them, tell them I'll scout around for another —"

"Ben — you dead set on this?" Ragland broke in anxiously. "You sure you won't reconsider even if the ante's raised?"

16

"I'm sure," Keenlyn replied, and, turning on a heel, headed back into the house.

Pete Amber watched the young rancher wheel about, his high, square shoulders silhouetting against the white-washed front of the house. He swore and jerked his horse around savagely.

"Let's get the hell out of here," he snapped to the others.

The riders wheeled in a tight group. Ed Suber reached into his saddlebags and took out a bottle. "Never figured Ben to be so goddamn bullheaded," he said, taking a long pull at the liquor.

Hensley mopped at his face. "Made him the best offer I could — more than the place is worth, really. But I was thinking of the deal as a whole."

"Keep thinking about it," Pete Amber said harshly. "Just hold your people off for a bit, tell them keep their britches on. This Keenlyn'll see things my way or he'll find himself in the goddamnedest war he ever heard of!"

III

Keenlyn paused in the doorway as Aaron Cash emerged from the tamarisk. Two distinct clicks sounded in the amber twilight as the old puncher released the hammers of his shotgun.

"Should've used this," he grumbled as he came up onto the porch. "That Jack — dose of buckshot'd maybe learn him some manners, talking like he did."

"About all it amounted to," Ben said.

Cash propped the weapon against the wall and shook his head. "Don't you go figuring him short now. He's a real handy-andy with that fancy hogleg he's carrying. And Gabe Carlin and some of them others Amber calls a crew'll side with him at the drop of a hat."

"Jack'll do just what Pete tells him."

"Maybe. He's hoping to be a big man like his pa someday. That kind of thinking could make him do something foolish."

Ben stared thoughtfully after the riders, now topping out the last roll of land before the main road. Was this the end of it — or just the beginning? he wondered.

"Ain't sure how you're looking at things," the old puncher said, "but I'm saying we got us a passel of trouble. Pete Amber ain't done — not by a damn sight."

Keenlyn sighed heavily. "Yes. Guess you're right."

"Know I'm right! Ain't nobody ever bucked Pete before. Way he figures he's standing one notch below God Almighty himself and just aching to take the next step up. Can't believe there's somebody around who won't jump and holler frog when he points a finger."

Ben was silent. Back in the kitchen Casimiro was rattling pans as he prepared the evening meal. The aged Mexican had been with Ben's father since the start, just as Aaron Cash had.

"Be smart to get things set," the old rider said. "Sure don't pay to get caught with your boots off."

Keenlyn nodded. "Expect the first thing to do is tell the others. Where are they?"

"Jess Homan's watching that bunch of cows we got up close to the creek. Buck's camping in the line shack over near the bluffs. Chet's down on the south range with the rest of the stock."

"We'll change that tomorrow," Keenlyn said. "Start a gather, drive the whole herd into that big meadow east of the creek, keep them in one bunch. Be easier to guard."

Cash bobbed his head. "For a fact. Boys can scatter out. With us helping, that Seven

Bar bunch won't get a chance to pull off anything — but you can figure they'll try. Old
Pete's ornery."

"And plenty mad."

Aaron grinned, slapped his hands together.
"That's for danged sure! Ain't never seen him
that put out. Expect it was the first time anybody plain told him to go to hell."

"He knew how I felt about selling out. Made
it clear at that meeting, but they insisted I
think it over. Shouldn't have been any surprise."

"Pete's way of doing things. Figured if you
sweat it out for a spell, you'd get to worrying
about what might happen if you didn't string
along with him."

"Good chance it might end here," Ben said.
"Don't think Hensley wants any trouble.
Probably drop it, find some other place."

Cash shifted on his feet, stroked his stringy
mustache. "Could be he'd like to, but Pete'll
never let him. He's aching to sell Seven Bar,
same as Suber and Homer Ragland are their
places. And there ain't nothing he won't do
to get his way. Don't fool yourself into figuring he'll back off."

Keenlyn glanced at the older man. "You
think I ought to sell?"

Cash shook his head violently. "Now, dang
it, I never said that! Ain't even thinking it.

Just want you to be sure you know what you're buying into."

"You want to pull out before it starts — if it does?"

Ben regretted his words instantly, knowing they cut deep. Aaron Cash looked away, his old eyes gazing out over the darkening land. "I ain't about to do that, son," he said softly.

Keenlyn laid his hand on the older man's shoulder. "Forget I even asked," he murmured. "Guess I'm a bit worked up — worried about something Pete said."

Aaron's ragged brows lifted questioningly.

"That things would go hard on anybody that was friendly with me."

Cash swore. "Like Pete to hit at a man that way. But I wouldn't worry none. This'll separate the friends from them that claims they are."

"Sol Seligman — he's the one I'm afraid —"

"Don't fret none over Sol. He's the kind that was old and wise even before he was born. Sol can handle Pete seven days a week and have time to spare."

"Sort of hate it because of Homer Ragland too. He was counting on the sale so he and his wife could move away."

Cash snorted. "That woman! Fair sets a man afire — even an old bonerack like me — and she knows it! No matter where Homer takes her it'll always be the same story. Wanting this, wanting that — giving him no peace. Was he smart he'd send her packing, but he won't. She's got a hold on him like a bald eagle carrying off a rabbit."

Aaron paused, peered closely at Ben. "Heard him mention the little gal. This going to make things bad for you two?"

"Don't know. Won't be easy for her. Thought I'd take a ride over to Ragland's tomorrow, see how she feels about it."

"Expect she'll stand by you," the old puncher said firmly. "Good stuff in her."

"Feels she owes Homer something, taking her in like he did."

"Reckon she's paid that favor back a long time ago. From what I hear that Emerald ain't much at doing anything 'cepting laying around, keeping herself all gussied up for the hired hands to gawk at. . . . Some talk about her and Ragland's foreman, George Rusk —"

"Just talk," Ben cut in. "Be going into town tomorrow, too, for supplies. Anything you need?"

"Chawing and smoking tobacco's about all. Won't hurt none to buy up a few boxes of cartridges."

Ben Keenlyn nodded soberly. "I'll tend to it," he said, and moved on into the house.

22

IV

When Ben Keenlyn arrived in Ute Springs the next morning the first thing to draw his attention was the big yellow stallion Pete Amber rode. Standing with the rancher's horse were two others. Jack Amber's sorrel and a bay bearing the Seven Bar brand. Gabe Carlin's, he supposed.

Ben grinned tightly as he swung his buckboard into Seligman's wagon yard. Parking the light rig behind Seligman's, he cut back around the side and came into the dusty street. There were only a few persons abroad. The rocking chairs on the porch of Moriarity's Hotel were deserted, and only a few horses waited at Tiffany's Saloon. It was one of those lazy mornings, hot early, with dust already hanging in a thin tan haze on the still air.

Ben stepped up onto the sidewalk of planks and slowed as the Ambers, Gorman Hensley, and Gabe Carlin came from the bank. All saw him immediately and halted.

Pete Amber's face was flushed, betraying the anger that possessed him. Evidently his visit to the banker had been in connection with the Box K, and the discovery that the ranch's mortgage was paid was irking him deeply.

"Save your breath," Keenlyn drawled. "Nothing's changed."

"Better listen," Pete Amber snapped. "Ain't often I give a man a second chance. Just don't figure you know what you're letting yourself in for."

"Meaning?"

The rancher made an indefinite motion at the buildings lining the street. "Meaning you ain't going to find no friends around here. Folks were plenty upset when they found out you were against them."

Temper stirred Keenlyn. Apparently the Ambers had been up bright and early passing along the word — and planting their subtle threats.

"They feel that way, it's their privilege," he said stiffly. "Always do my buying in some other town."

"Getting back home with it'll be something else," Jack Amber observed dryly.

"Try stopping me," Ben said. "Be the last thing you'll ever do."

"Oh, I don't know," Jack continued. "Expect you're plenty long on talk, not much on anything else." He winked broadly at his father and the other men. "Expect was I of a mind to take time, I could make you see the light same as my pa did yours."

Keenlyn's jaw hardened as he took a step

24

nearer Jack. "What's my pa got to do with this?"

"Well, there's that old saying, like father, like son. Expect it'll run true. When Pa decided to trail his herds across your pa's land, he just done it. Was no argument."

"Only because he had permission — an agreement."

"You're a little mixed up. Was because your old man was afraid not to let him. Had a yellow streak up —"

Ben hit Jack Amber hard across the mouth, sent him staggering back. Jack's hand swept down for the gun on his hip. Keenlyn slapped it away, drove a second blow to Amber's jaw.

Carlin yelled something, but Pete Amber, some secret thought in his devious mind, simply stood back, watching with a sly grin. Two men who had been in front of Hoffman's Feed Store were approaching at a run, and back up the street again Town Marshal Floyd Melrose was hurrying through the loose dust.

Jack, half-crouched, knees quivering slightly from the shock of Keenlyn's knotted fist, threw a glance to his pistol lying a few paces away. He wheeled suddenly to recover it. Ben crossed swiftly and smashed another right to the man's head, dropping him to all fours. A motion to the side brought him around sharply. The half smile had died on

Pete Amber's lips. Gabe Carlin was easing around to get in behind him.

"Take a hand in this and I'll kill you!" Ben snarled savagely, his own fingers dropping to the pistol on his hip.

Carlin froze, shook his head, and began to back off. Seething with fury, Keenlyn reached down, grasped Jack by the shirt front, and dragged him half-upright. Holding the limp figure erect, he drove another hard blow into the man's jaw, then stepped back, allowing him to fall.

Ben's set face swung to Pete Amber. "I ever hear of him telling that lie again he'll get a chance to use that fancy gun of his! Understand?"

The rancher simply stared. Abruptly he wheeled and, ignoring Jack's prostrate shape, stalked toward his horse. There was no sound from the small crowd that had accumulated, but Melrose, just reaching the circle, broke the hush.

"What's going on here? What's this all about?"

Ben jerked his head impatiently at Pete Amber. "Ask him," he said, brushing at the sweat on his face.

The old lawman frowned, glanced to where Carlin and Hensley were helping Jack to his feet and then to Pete Amber's broad back.

But he voiced no question; he simply stood there looking back and forth uncertainly.

"Pete!" Keenlyn called in a voice that still trembled with anger. "Giving you notice here and now. My range is closed to you beginning today. The agreement my pa made you is off."

The rancher did not turn around. One hand on the saddle horn, the other on the cantle, he hung motionless for a long minute and then completed his swing onto the stallion. Ben, anger beginning to drain from his heaving frame, wheeled, stepped back up onto the walk. Pete Amber's sardonic tones reached him.

"Could be you won't have nothing to say about that — or anything else."

Anger ripped afresh through Keenlyn. Taut, shoulders a hard, straight line, he stepped up onto Seligman's porch and pushed his way into the building.

The merchant was standing just inside the door. He had witnessed the incident. Nerves still raw, Keenlyn confronted the lean-faced man.

"I'm here for supplies. You want my business?"

Sol studied the angry features of the young rancher briefly and shrugged. "When such a day comes I will tell you. To ask there will be no need."

The stiffness faded from Keenlyn's frame. There was no sense venting his rage on Sol — probably the only friend he had in Ute Springs. "Sorry," he murmured. "Don't mean to take it out on you."

Seligman smiled. "You have a list?"

Ben reached into his shirt pocket for his list and handed it to the merchant.

"Not sure you ought to do this," he said. "Don't want to get you in trouble with Amber."

"The world is full of Pete Ambers," Seligman said in a resigned sort of way. "If a man bows to one, he'll spend his life bowing to the others. It is no way to live." He turned away and began to assemble the items on the list. When he came to the cartridges, he paused. "Always the answer is this — to shoot," he said, and then proceeded to select the ammunition from his stock.

As Ben drove the wagon homeward, his mind returned again to the merchant. Pete Amber could make things hard for the old man, force others to boycott —

Abruptly, his thoughts came to a full stop. Far ahead a huge pall of dark smoke hung over the land west of the Feather Mountains — his land! Fear caught at his throat. . . . Fire sweeping through the dry brush and range grass, trapping cattle — there was nothing worse.

Leaning forward, anxiety gripping him, he began to ply the whip.

V

Keenlyn rushed into the Box K yard in a swirl of dust. Instantly the back door of the house burst open, and Casimiro, one hand clutching at the apron knotted around his waist, pointed excitedly at the boiling smoke with the other.

Ben only nodded, pulled the buckboard to a sliding halt. Leaping from the seat he lifted the box of supplies out, set it on the ground, and vaulted back into the vehicle. Face grim, he struck off across the flat for the ugly smudge darkening the sky.

The thick clouds had shifted and seemed now to be drifting toward the mountains. The breeze had changed, he realized, and he heaved a grateful sigh. The fire, reaching the rocky base of the Feathers, would quickly burn itself out. But that wouldn't compensate for the damage done.

He saw Jess Homan a few minutes later. The young puncher's face was streaked with soot, and there were places in his clothing where sparks had fallen. Slumped on his saddle, eyes reflecting his weariness, Jess pulled up to the buckboard and stopped.

"Reckon things are all right now, Mr. Keenlyn. Was mighty close there for a spell.

Sure glad that wind changed."

"You look like you had it pretty bad. How about the others?"

"Don't rightly know about them. Last I seen of Buck and Aaron they was over there, heading in behind them trees."

"We lose any cattle?"

Homan shook his head. "Lucky there, too. Aaron had us up moving them out first thing this morning. Chet's down near the creek with them right now."

Ben settled back, relieved. No one had got hurt; no steers had been lost. He glanced toward the hills. Smoke was thinning rapidly now.

"Where'd it start?" he asked.

Jess pulled off his hat, scratched at his thick mass of cottony hair. "Up the ways apiece, I guess. Was already moving fast this way when I come up to lend a hand. . . . Aaron and Buck's coming now. Expect they can tell you."

Keenlyn turned his attention to a small stand of trees off to the left. Two riders had rounded the end of the grove and were moving up at a lope. Like Homan, they bore the marks of their encounter with the fire.

Aaron's features were solemn as he pulled to a stop, sleeved the sweat from his eyes, and said, "Well, I reckon it's started. Me and

31

Buck can show you right where some yahoo built hisself half a dozen fires, then scattered 'em so's things would get to going fast."

"Was somebody what knowed we had stock grazing down in the hollow," Aaron said. "Fire was figured to trap them. Sure proud we moved them out first thing this morning. . . . And I reckon there ain't no doubt who that somebody is. Only Pete or Jack Amber'd stoop to a trick like that."

"Wasn't either one of them. Or Carlin. Ran into all three in town this morning."

"Ain't no proof they didn't get things all fixed ahead of time with some of the crew."

Ben nodded. "You find any tracks?"

Cash clawed at his chin. "Never thought to look. Found where them fires was set, then seen you coming across the flat. Was so mad I hurried to tell you about it."

"Let's go back there," Keenlyn said, cutting the buckboard around. He swung his attention to Jess Homan and Buck Grimmer. "Obliged to you both."

The younger man grinned. Buck shrugged. "We're Box K. Reckon it was our job. You want us tagging along? If not, expect we'd better start drifting the rest of the beef toward the creek."

"Go ahead," Ben said. "And I'm thanking you again."

Grimmer touched the frayed brim of his hat with a forefinger and pulled away, followed closely by Jess Homan.

Aaron Cash watched them briefly, then clucked. "Mighty good boys. Sure hope nothing happens to them."

"Nothing had better happen to them," Keenlyn said quietly.

Cash squinted at the young rancher. "Something besides this here fire got you riled up?"

"Had a little run-in with the Ambers in town, that's all. Show me where those fires started."

The old rider pulled away, angling across the shallow basin where they had halted. When they rounded the spur of trees that trickled out from the hills, Ben had his first broad glimpse of the blackened, smoking path the fire had taken.

It was a good quarter mile wide and extended all the way to the Feathers. The flames had consumed at least fifty acres of grass and brush. Temper rose again within him. . . . A hell of a way to fight a man — burn off his range, try to destroy his livestock. But as Aaron had remarked, that was the way Pete Amber would do it.

"Right over here," he heard the old rider say, and wheeled the buckboard around to where Cash had stopped and was waiting for him.

He dropped from the rig, stepped to Aaron's side. The fire had moved from that point, he saw.

"Was a pretty fair-sized fire started here," Aaron said. "You'll find more places, littler than this one, strung along for a couple hundred yards."

"Look for tracks," Ben said.

He found what he sought a short time later. Two horses had waited beside a clump of cedars some fifty yards back of where the larger fire had been laid. The hoofprints showed that the riders had come in from the west and gone back the same direction.

Only Pete Amber's Seven Bar lay to the west. Ben turned to Aaron. "I'm borrowing your horse. Take the buckboard back to the ranch."

The old puncher frowned. "Where you going?"

"Seven Bar. Got a few things I want to say to Pete."

Aaron shook his head doubtfully. "Ain't so sure that'd be smart — feeling like you do. Best you wait, cool off."

"No point in waiting," Ben said, swinging onto the saddle of the bay. "Be no different later."

"Then I reckon I'd better come along, sort of side you."

"Getting the herd moved to a safe place is more important right now. That's where you're needed most — with Buck and the others."

Cash grunted, turned to the buckboard. "You're the boss-man, but you'd better get it into your head you can't do the fighting alone. Going to need help."

"Know that," Keenlyn replied, the edge of his tone softening. "But this will be no fight, only talk."

"That's what you're hoping. Downright foolish you riding in there alone. Odds'll be twenty to one. Worse, maybe."

"Won't be any less tomorrow or the next day. I'm not going looking for trouble — just aim to tell Pete I know how the fire started, warn him it had better not happen again."

Aaron Cash wheeled slowly, his weathered face bleak. "Them ain't fighting words?"

"That's up to Pete," Ben said, and rode on.

VI

Still smoldering, Keenlyn rode through Seven Bar's tall gate and a short time later halted in front of the low, rambling ranch house. Pete had been fairly well off financially when he moved into the valley, Ben had been told, and had gone to considerable expense building himself a fine place.

Amber had watched him approach. He stood in the doorway, his big frame filling the opening for a brief time as he studied Keenlyn. Then he stepped out onto the porch.

"Well?" he demanded in a surly voice.

Keenlyn bristled and his anger heightened, but he remained perfectly still on the saddle, both hands in view. From the corner of his eye he saw two Seven Bar men slide quietly into view at the corner of the house on his right; three more appeared at the opposite side. All halted, merely stood, arms crossed, watching.

"Northeast corner of my range was fired today," Ben said.

Pete Amber leaned against a roof support, a faint smirk on his broad face. "Why're you telling me?"

"Cost me some grass. Cattle had all been moved."

"Lucky," the rancher grunted.

"Other way around," Ben said evenly. "Lucky for you."

"Your beef, not mine."

"But you would have paid for it. I'd have come here to collect."

The rancher straightened, cocked his head to one side. "You saying I had something to do with it? You got any proof?"

"No doubt of it — but no proof. Tracks came from your range, headed back the same way. In my book that means some of your bunch — two men — set the fire."

Amber shrugged his thick shoulders, glanced sideways to the men gathered at each end of the house. A hush had fallen over the yard.

"You got a lot of guts coming here, accusing me," Pete said. "I ought to —"

"Blame goes where it belongs," Ben broke in coolly. "And if that's a move aimed to make me sell, you're wasting time."

Amber's face darkened, and he took a half step forward. Keenlyn, constantly aware of the men at the corners of the house, remained still. He'd give them no excuse to go for their guns.

"It happens again," he continued, "I'll be

37

paying you in kind. Better understand that, too."

Nodding curtly, he wheeled the bay around. Placing his back to Amber and his men, he headed for the distant gate. Tension gripped him, and the hair along his neck prickled. He was taking a hell of a chance, gambling that Pete Amber, with all his faults, still would not shoot a man down from behind. . . .

He reached the gate after what seemed an interminable time, breathed deeper, and looked over his shoulder. Pete was yet on the porch. He'd been joined by several other men — Gorman Hensley, Jack, and a couple of others. The crew members had closed in, were now gathered directly in front of the house.

He'd figured Pete right, and he'd had his say, he thought as he pointed the bay east for the Ragland place. Amber knew now that he'd get a fight if he wanted it. Now maybe he'd drop it; maybe he'd realize he couldn't force the sale of the Box K.

But down in his heart Ben Keenlyn doubted it. Pete Amber was the sort of man who'd have his way — or else.

Marcie, crisp and cool in a blue-and-white dress, met him as he rode into Ragland's yard. Her head was uncovered, and the sunlight caught her blonde hair and turned it pale gold.

It looked like a crown, Ben thought as he swung up to the hitchrack and dismounted.

She came to him at once and kissed him lightly on the cheek, but there was restraint in her manner and soberness to her soft features. Problems with Emerald, he supposed as he smiled down at her.

"Things worse than usual?"

She shook her head and, taking him by the hand, led him to the bench that had been built around the trunk of a huge, spreading cottonwood.

"About the same, I suppose," she said then. "Emerald's never let up on Uncle Homer."

Ben shrugged. "Expect I'm not going to be very welcome around here, seeing as how I'm the big stumbling block in their way."

Marcie looked up into his wind-burned face. "Uncle Homer said you'd refused. Is there a chance you'll change your mind?"

"No," he said flatly, and then frowned. "Why? Do you want me to?"

The girl sighed. "I want you to do what you think's best — what suits you. Only . . ."

She let her words trail off. Keenlyn rode out the pause and then, faintly angered, looked at her. "Only . . . ?"

"There seems to be so much trouble in the air — so much hate. I heard what happened

in town this morning. . . . You and Jack Amber
. . . the others."

"They asked for it."

"I — I know . . . I'm afraid, Ben — afraid
of what might happen to you if you don't go
along."

"Trouble's always around, one shape or another," he said. "Is it going to make any difference between us?"

"No, of course not," she replied quickly.
"But it would be so much easier for us all
if you'd agree. We could get married, take
the money — go somewhere else and buy a
ranch."

Disappointment stirred through him. "Got
a fine ranch now. Be a fool to give it up, start
over again. And I don't take kindly to running."

"But you'd still be alive!" Marcie said in
a low, desperate tone. "That's what matters
to me."

"Can look out for myself," he said stub-
bornly. "And that land agent Hensley — he's
not looking to start a fight."

"But Pete Amber is. He'll stop at nothing."

"Maybe. Just came from there. Had a little
talk with him. I think we understand each
other now."

Marcie turned and stared at Keenlyn incred-
ulously. "You went to Seven Bar?"

40

"Dropped by on my way over to see you."

"That's what I mean!" she cried in a sudden burst of exasperation. "You don't seem to realize the danger you're in! Why did you take a chance like that?"

"Somebody — a couple of his hired hands — set fire to my north range this morning. No big damage. Had to go by, tell him I knew he was behind it, warn him not to try it again."

Marcie stirred despondently. "I just can't make you understand."

"I'll be all right," he said, patting her hand. "Now, don't suppose you could scare up a bite to eat for a hungry man, could you? Been a long time since breakfast."

Marcie rose to her feet. "And it's almost suppertime!" she scolded. "When will you learn to eat regularly?"

"When you move into my place and take charge," he grinned, and followed her into the house.

Emerald Ragland was in the parlor, dressed to perfection, hair carefully arranged, a faint glow of rouge on her cheeks. Her large, green-shadowed eyes greeted Keenlyn with cool reserve, and her exquisitely molded lips parted only slightly when she spoke.

"Good afternoon."

He nodded. "Glad to see you again, Mrs. Ragland."

41

Immediately she resumed reading the book she held, making it plain she had no further words for him. Marcie, holding his hand, continued on to the kitchen.

Pointing to a chair, she reached for a cup and saucer, and poured him a measure of coffee. As he sat down to enjoy that, she procured bread and sliced meat from a window box, along with a generous wedge of dried-apricot pie spread thick with butter.

"You could wait and take supper with us," Marcie said, sitting down opposite him.

He shook his head. "Doubt if that would be very comfortable for any of us."

"No, I guess not," she murmured.

"Where's Homer?"

"On the range somewhere. Left right after dinner. Didn't hear him say just where he was going."

Ragland could have been one of the men he'd seen at Amber's and been unable to distinguish, Ben thought. If true, some sort of meeting was probably in progress. He hoped so. They'd all have heard what he said, and they'd know he was willing to fight.

An hour later he mounted and, avoiding the road, cut south across Ragland's range for his ranch. The sun was already lowering, and he could save considerable time by taking a direct route. Ragland's grass looked good, he noted idly as he rode steadily on. Arrowhead was a fine spread. Too bad Emerald was so dead set on forcing Homer to give it all up.

At dusk, he reached the line of trees that marked the north boundary of his property. It was pleasant among the cottonwoods and sycamores. The heat was gone, and birds chirped softly as they settled down for the night. It was good to be alive in such a country, to have his own land, to look forward to the day when Marcie would become a part of his life, enjoy the things he —

The sudden spiteful crack of a rifle jarred him to abrupt awareness. Bits of leather exploded from his saddle as the bullet ripped into the cantle. In the next instant he was leaving his horse in a low dive, seeking safety in the brush along the trail.

VII

Keenlyn hit hard. Breath exploded from his lungs, and pain stabbed through him as a shoulder came against a rock. The rifle spoke again, the bullet showering him with dirt. Desperate, he threw himself to one side.

A third shot echoed through the grove. Cursing, Keenlyn rolled away, dragging out his pistol as he moved, all the while trying to locate the bushwhacker. The hidden marksman fired twice in rapid succession. He could hear the vicious clipping sound the slugs made as they tore through the leaves of the mountain mahogany behind him.

Sweat pouring off him, he reversed himself, lunged, and gained the protection of a small log. No bullets had followed that move, and he lay still, panting. Moments dragged into minutes. Cautiously he raised his head. Had the ambusher pulled out?

Two more shots crashed through the hush, splintering the log behind which Keenlyn lay. Turned suddenly furious by his own helplessness, Ben leaped to his feet and raced for a dense thicket of closely growing trees a dozen strides distant. He knew he was a fair target, but anything was better than squirming around in the dirt.

The rifleman was watching closely. Instantly he pressed off a shot. Ben heard the lead slap into a cottonwood directly behind him. He veered sharp left, doubled right. Bullets tracked his every move with relentless determination, but he gained the thicket and plunged into the protection of sturdy trunks. He was breathing hard, and sweat clouded his eyes, but grim satisfaction was now flowing through him. He'd made it — and more, he had located the hidden marksman, or at least knew his general position.

Crouched, he peered through the falling darkness toward a low embankment a hundred yards or so away. He could see no sign of the killer, but the last muzzle flash had been almost in direct center. Simply to start firing would serve only to betray his own position. The range was much too far for a pistol.

Drawing back, he looked around for his horse. Frightened by the first burst of gunshots, the animal had shied off into the brush. He located the bay standing some distance to his right, barely visible among the trees. Keenlyn swore softly. He could forget about the rifle hanging from the saddle.

He swung his attention back to the ridge. By following out the band of trees he was in, he could approach the embankment from its end and very possibly work his way around until he was in behind the ambusher. In a few more minutes it would be dark enough to make a try. One thing sure — he wasn't going to stay pinned down there in the thicket all night.

Somebody wanted him dead. . . .

That conclusion was not hard to reach, and who that somebody might be was equally simple to figure out — Pete Amber. He'd been a fool to think the rancher's reaction would be anything else.

A pale moonlit darkness took over the land, turning it hazy and silver, lending an eerie quality, but the shadows were broad and deep. Pistol in hand, Ben began to move forward, working his way from one dark area to another, moving as silently as possible.

A short time later he pulled up short as the distant racketing of gunshots carried through the hush. Immediate concern gripped him. The reports had come from the south — from the general direction of his own range. . . . Something was happening there — a raid, perhaps.

He could do nothing to help. He'd never reach the bay, not with the bushwhacker just waiting for him to take a step into the open. Harsh tension flaying his nerves, he pushed on through the brush at a quickened pace.

Gaining the first rise of the embankment he halted, listened. Gunshots, faint and marching in a steady procession, still hung in the distance. But they seemed nearer and more to the east, not coming from the area where the ranch house and other buildings stood, as he had thought at first.

His throat tightened. Cattle were on that part of his range. Aaron and the crew would not have had time to move them off yet, as he had ordered.

An impatient curse ripped from his lips. He had to get down there fast. Taut, he dropped low, began to work his way hurriedly up the ridge, the sporadic pop of faraway rifles a jabbing spur in his sides.

He gained a high point on the embankment, dropped behind a clump of cedar, and looked ahead. . . . Rocks . . . deep shadows . . . brushy clumps. Edgy, he cut around and began to move along the back rim of the ridge. The bushwhacker should be close. The center of the formation was now to his left, only paces away. But where —

A blinding flash of light and a deafening crash of thunder came together. Keenlyn staggered, fell hard, his own weapon discharging as he struck the ground. Angered, he rolled away, sprang to his feet. He had all but stepped on the hiding man!

Crouched, Ben listened into the silence. Nothing. After a time he moved cautiously to his right, toward a large boulder poised on the edge of the ridge. From there he could look upon the face of the embankment, have the rock as protection.

He halted, drew himself upright as the quick drumbeat of a running horse racing away reached him. The bushwhacker was calling it quits, either wounded by a lucky accidental shot or having had his fill of the nerve-racking duel in the night.

Wheeling, Ben came off the ridge at a hard run, caught up the bay, and, swinging to the saddle, headed for the distant gunshots.

VIII

He broke out of the trees at a dead gallop, recklessly cutting in and out of the brush clumps, scrub cedars, and junipers, plunging down into sandy arroyos, up their opposite sides.

The shooting was continuing, not as much as earlier, but still a steady crackling in the night. As Ben drew nearer, his apprehension grew. Whatever was happening, Aaron Cash and the rest of his small crew were apparently unable to stop it.

Minutes later he reached the edge of the badlands, swept down into a small basin. This was where part of the beef had been pastured, and at once he saw, vague in the distance, a shadowy mass that could only be running cattle. Ahead dark shapes lay scattered here and there on the grass. To his right a dozen or more riders, silhouetted in the night, were veering back and forth, shooting into the fleeing herd.

An oath exploded from Ben Keenlyn's lips. Raiders were slaughtering his stock, killing the steers as they ran. And then cold fear tightened his throat. His crew — where were they? Had they been shot down too?

Drawing his pistol he cut hard right and rode straight for the weaving, yelling raiders. Long before he was within range, he opened up, firing directly at the riders, knowing the bullets would fall short but hopeful of distracting them and stopping the senseless slaughter.

His move had the desired effect. The raiders, possibly thinking that several men were coming in, swung off, drove hard for a low ridge to the west. Anger spurring him on, Keenlyn gave chase, closing the gap slightly but never drawing near enough to make his shots count.

When he finally gained the ridge the men had disappeared into the night. Worried, disconsolate, he doubled back toward the herd. He'd lost heavily, he knew, but his main concern was for Aaron and the others. Had all four men . . . ?

Relief flowed through him as he saw two riders loom up in the half dark. Roweling the tired bay, he rushed forward to meet them. It was Aaron Cash and the youngster Jess Homan.

The old puncher, hawk face set to grim lines, greeted him with a hopeless shake of his head. "Hell of a thing. Done the best we could, but they was just too many of them. . . . And Buck's dead."

Keenlyn stiffened. "How?"

"We was trying to swing the stampede toward the hills. Buck was sort of in the front. Horse must've stumbled. Fell. Reckon about half the critters in the herd stomped on him."

The surging fury and hatred within Ben Keenlyn settled into a cold, pulsing force. "Recognize any of the raiders?"

"Was masked, and we never did get close to any of them anyways. They was careful about that. Was I guessing, I'd say there was waddies there from every ranch in the valley, with Seven Bar leading the pack."

That would be the way Pete Amber would do it. He'd spearhead the attack but see to it that each rancher had at least one man in the party.

"Expect we lost forty, maybe fifty head," Cash said, brushing at his haggard, dust-streaked face.

"Where's Grimmer's body?" Ben asked.

"Chet loaded him up — what was left — took him to the ranch. Sure wisht we could've saved some of them steers."

"Not blaming you for anything. Did all anybody could have done. Figured to be here earlier myself, only I got held up."

Aaron scrubbed at his jaw. "Pete try something?"

"Was a bushwhacker waiting for me up near

51

the line. Expect he was part of the bunch that hit the herd."

The old puncher nodded. "Would've knowed you'd be coming that way after you left Ragland's. Get a look at him?"

"Hardly at all," Ben said. "Pinned me down with a rifle. I finally got loose, tried sneaking up on him, but he got away. Could be I winged him."

Cash sighed. "Too bad he ain't dead. Know who he was then and have us some proof to throw in Pete's face."

"Got all the proof I want," Ben said grimly. "In my mind, anyway."

"Mr. Keenlyn," Jess Homan said.

Ben turned to the young puncher. Homan was badly shaken. In the pale light the skin was pulled tight over the bones of his face, giving it a skull-like appearance.

"I'm quitting," Jess said. "Figured I'd best tell you now."

Aaron Cash spun to the boy. "You're doing what?"

"Quitting. Don't want to get mixed up in no war. And seeing what happened to Buck, I —"

"You letting them scare you off?" Aaron demanded, his voice thick with sarcasm.

"Not that. I just don't aim —"

"It's all right," Keenlyn said. Persuading

the young puncher to stay would serve no good purpose. Feeling as he did he'd be of little use and could never be depended upon.

"I understand. Ride in to the ranch. I'll meet you later, pay you what you've got coming."

"Ain't much," Homan mumbled. "If it's all the same to you, I'll just pick up my duds and gear and move on."

"Suit yourself."

Immediately Homan swung around and loped off into the darkness.

"Never figured that boy'd turn tail," Aaron muttered. "Plumb yellow."

Keenlyn shrugged. "Could be he's the only one of us that's showing good sense."

"Nope. Man lets the likes of Pete Amber get away with something like this, he —"

"He's not getting away with it," Ben cut in quietly. "I warned him."

"What can you do about it? Ain't but you and me and Chet left. And old Casimiro. Not a drop in the bucket when it comes to going up against Pete's bunch."

"Won't take but one man to handle what I'm figuring to do. Told Pete if he tried anything, I'd pay him back."

"Alone? You're looney, boy!"

"Best thing you can do is go on in, get yourself some rest," Keenlyn said. "I'll be back by morning."

Aaron studied Ben quietly for a time, then shook his head. "Nope. You ain't goin' alone. I'm trailing right along with you."

Keenlyn considered. The herd would be safe, at least for the remainder of the night. "All right," he said. "Let's get started. But if anything goes wrong, you do what I tell you. That clear?"

"Sure is," Aaron said with a knowing smile, and patted the rifle hanging from his saddle.

IX

They moved off at a slow pace. The horses were worn, and both men, up and on the go since sunrise, dozed continually on the saddle.

Well after midnight they halted atop the ridge above Amber's Seven Bar spread. Lamplight glowed in one window of the main house and in those of the low-roofed structure where the crew bunked.

There was no activity in the yard or around the corrals, and Keenlyn guessed the men who had participated in the raid on his herd were turning in. Likely the leaders of the bunch were in the main house making their report to Pete. That would account for his still being up.

Aaron groaned wearily and shifted on his horse. "Now what? Looking ain't getting us nowhere."

"Sit tight. Waiting for the lights to go out."

"Then what?"

"Pete Amber's going to get his taste of fire."

The old puncher's jaw sagged. "You burning him out?"

"Be up to him and how fast his crew can put out the flames. I'm hoping they'll be slow."

Cash slapped his leg joyfully. "This is sure going to be something a man can write home about!"

"There goes the main house," Ben said.

Amber's men had apparently made their report. The window was suddenly dark, and a few moments later two shadows crossed the yard to the bunkhouse. A rectangle of yellow light flashed as a door was opened.

"Fair breeze coming from the north," Aaron commented as they waited, eyes on the windows of the crew's quarters.

"Be the side to work from," Ben answered. Then, as darkness claimed the bunkhouse, he added, "Let's get at it."

Following the ridge, they rode across the rear of Seven Bar, cut right, and made their way to the northern edge of the basin. Uncoiling his rope, Ben shook out a loop, began to drag up what dead brush he could find, and piled it against the weathered poles of a corral that formed the outer boundary of the yard. Aaron Cash, taking his cue from Keenlyn, pitched in to help.

It took the better part of an hour. Ben wanted the entire length of the fence banked. The job finally completed, they drew up near the center. Wiping sweat from his face, Ben explained the plan.

Cash nodded his understanding. Then,

"Which way'll we head? Five minutes after that fire starts there'll be Seven Bar all over this side of the mountain!"

"Same way we came in — back along the ridge. There'll be plenty of Pete's bunch around, all right, but they're going to be so busy they'll have no time to look for us. Ready?"

"Just like a kid waiting to set off a firecracker. Expect you know Pete Amber ain't going to let this pass."

"I know," Keenlyn said, "but he'll be realizing something too."

"What's that?"

"We can both play this kind of a game."

Abruptly he whirled away toward the end farthest from the ridge, leaving the shorter distance to safety for Aaron. Reaching the end of the fence, he dropped to the ground. Searching about briefly, he picked up a dozen thoroughly dry branches. Turning his back to the distant buildings in order to shield the glare, he struck a match. The first branch caught instantly. Laying it down, he held the others over it until all were blazing and he had a handful of torches.

Climbing back onto the bay, he came about and started for the center of the brush-packed line, tossing powder-dry brush every ten feet or so. At the opposite end he could see Aaron

Cash working toward him, depositing his firebrands in similar fashion.

When they met in center the ends were already blazing strong, and in one place the dancing tongues had already licked through the fence and were beginning to race across the tinderlike grass.

Keenlyn beckoned to Cash, and together they doubled back for the ridge. They kept to the low side, but there was little chance of their being seen. A thick pall of smoke was rolling down into the basin, engulfing the buildings of Seven Bar. Everything behind it was obscured.

They reached the point west of the ranch where they had paused earlier and here they stopped. The air was hot and filled with an ominous crackling that caused the horses, despite their weariness, to fidget. Flames now surrounded all the fence poles, and more fire had crossed the narrow grass-covered interval separating the corral from the yard proper. It was beginning to snap hungrily at the walls of the first sheds.

"The smoke — they've got a whiff of it," Keenlyn said, pointing.

Lights had come on in the bunkhouse, showing dimly through the swirling pall. Others appeared — the small structure the foreman occupied and one adjacent to the barn used by the hostlers. And finally the main house.

"Reckon we got them all up," Aaron Cash said dryly.

Ben nodded soberly. "Expect so," he said. "Let's go home."

X

First light was showing beyond the crags and ridges of the Feather Mountains when they rode into the yard of the Box K. Casimiro, his dark face wreathed in a worried frown, came from the kitchen at once to greet them.

"Señores . . . I worry. . . ."

"We're all right," Ben said wearily. He was dead on his feet, but rest was out of the question, at least for a time. Pete Amber would strike back; how and when was the problem.

"The *muchacho,*" Casimiro said hesitantly. "He go."

Keenlyn nodded. "Not coming back. How about fixing us something to eat — plenty of strong coffee."

The old Mexican bobbed his head, wheeled, and hurried toward the house.

"Where's Chet?" Cash called after him.

"He go to the cattle," the cook answered, slowing. "Buck — he is in the barn. We did not know what to do."

Casimiro reached the house, entered. Aaron looked expectantly at Ben.

"We'll bury him out on the slope, where Pa is," Keenlyn said.

Cash smiled. "Right pleased you're doing

that instead of carting him off to the town's graveyard. Old Buck was a Box K man and proud of it."

After the battered, canvas-wrapped body of Grimmer had been laid in its grave and the freshly turned earth replaced, Ben stood for a moment looking down, lost in bitter thought. A good man was dead, thanks to Pete Amber's determination to have his way. Half a hundred steers had been senselessly slaughtered, fire and counterfire blackened the land — and the whirlwind of destruction had only begun. Who would be the next to die?

"Said I'd fix up a marker for Buck, first chance I get. . . ."

Keenlyn became aware of Aaron Cash's voice and nodded woodenly. Picking up the spade he had been using, he turned and started for the house.

Ben and Aaron ate hurriedly, and when the meal was over Keenlyn rose and faced the older man.

"Get some rest — three, four hours, at least. I'll spell Chet while he eats."

Aaron tipped back his chair. "Won't be no three, four hours before we hear from Pete Amber!"

"Depends. Don't think he'll make any move right off. He'll be wanting to make it look good as he can, like I finally forced him to act."

Aaron grinned broadly. "You don't figure burning down half his property ain't reason enough?"

"Doubt if we did that much damage. . . . Have to gamble on him not cracking down, anyway — leastwise today. Need time to get set."

"Fort up, you mean?"

"What it amounts to. I think the best thing is to drive the herd into that box canyon east of Bear Creek and hold them there."

"Ain't no water —"

"Know that, and we haven't got time to drive them back. Can't take the chance of getting caught in between. They can go a few days without."

"What'll we be doing after we get them in there?"

"Aim to set up camp inside the mouth of the canyon. Plenty of big rocks there. That way we'll keep the herd out of Amber's reach and be able to hold our own if it comes to shooting."

"Which it sure will," Cash said, glancing around the room. "What about this here house? We can't be in that canyon and here, too."

Ben Keenlyn turned away and stared

through the window. He'd been born here, had grown up in the structure built by his father. He'd known no other roof.

"Be hard to lose it," he murmured, "and I hope I don't. Only chance is that if he doesn't find us holed up here, he'll pass it by."

"Not Pete. He'll be out to wipe you clean off the face of the country."

Ben nodded in agreement. Abruptly he turned for the door, the need to get set for trouble filling him with sudden urgency. He paused, hearing Aaron Cash come to his feet. Frowning, he watched the old puncher reach for his hat.

"Told you to get some sleep."

"No need," Cash said cheerfully. "That there stuff Casimiro calls coffee'd put fight in a dead caterpillar. You're going to have to have help driving them critters into that canyon."

"They're not far from there."

"No difference. It'll take all three of us till noon."

Ben wasted no more time arguing. Every minute could be important. Hurrying to the barn with Cash at his side, he saddled a fresh horse, saw to his rifle, and then pulled aside to wait until Aaron had completed a similar chore. Shortly, they rode from the yard.

They found Chet hunched over a small fire

drinking coffee from a lard tin, the entire herd spread out over a broad flat below him.

"Ride in and get yourself some breakfast," Keenlyn told him. "I figure we're in for plenty of trouble, starting today. You feel like moving on, you're welcome."

Buntin jerked the reins of his horse free of the cedar to which they were looped and stood looking at the herd for a long minute.

"Reckon I'll just stick around," he said finally, and stepped to the saddle. "You fellows see that smoke north of here early this morning? Was a powerful lot of —"

"See it!" Aaron broke in with a wide grin. "Was us that started it! Paid a little visit to old Pete's last night, fixed him up a little something he could warm his toes with."

Buntin's usual stolid face cracked into a smile. "Well, I swan!" he murmured, and turned away. "Be right back — soon's I get a bite," he called over his shoulder. "Anything you want me to bring?"

"Plenty of cartridges for your rifle," Aaron said. "That there Texas Alamo ain't going to be nothing compared to what's liable to happen around here."

Chet considered that in his unresponsive way for a bit and then, nodding, rode on.

Ben and Cash began at once to get the herd moving. It would be no small task shifting fifteen hundred head of cattle into the narrow confines of the canyon.

By the time Chet Buntin returned, the first of the herd had reached the rocky entrance to the dead-end canyon and were trickling into its narrow width. Chet's presence enabled them to speed things up a bit, and near noon the three men halted in the mouth of the box; the last of the steers were inside.

It had been less of a job than Ben had anticipated, and some of the deep worry that had pressed him was fading. If Seven Bar decided to strike at his herd again, they'd find the cattle beyond reach.

"We setting up camp here?" Aaron asked, dismounting stiffly and rubbing at the muscles of his legs.

Keenlyn pointed to a small open area in the rocks. "Be a good place. Won't be seen from the flat. You can take turns catching up on your sleep."

"What'll you be doing?"

"Going back to the house. Few things I'd like to get, hide somewhere — just in case. And we'll be needing a little grub —"

"Ain't nobody doing nothing just yet," Buntin announced in his flat voice. "We got company."

XI

Keenlyn spun and looked down into the swale. A single rider was coming at a fast lope.

"Who is it?" Cash wondered, squinting through the spinning particles of dust hanging over the slope.

Ben was silent for a time, and then, as the approaching rider became more distinct, he said, "Marcie Ragland."

"The little gal? What's she doing here? Sure ain't no place for her — not with all the hellfire that's going to come hammering down on us."

Keenlyn moved forward of the two men, sharp concern flowing through him. Aaron was right. Marcie should not be exposing herself at a time like this. He halted and watched her pull up short and leap from the saddle.

"Oh, Ben," she cried in a thankful voice. "I made it in time! You've got to leave — get away!"

He caught her in his arms as she rushed to him. "Wait — slow down. Everything's all right."

"It's not all right! They're coming here, looking for you — Pete Amber and all the others. Even Uncle Homer."

"Been expecting Pete. We're ready."

"Ready!" she echoed, drawing back. "Ready to get killed!"

"Maybe not."

A sob wrenched from the girl's lips. She shook her head helplessly. "When will it end? After everyone in the valley is dead? Can't this all be settled some other way — not with guns and burnings and killings?"

"Up to Pete Amber and the others. No need for what's happening — and going to happen — but I can't run away."

"No," she said heavily, "you can't run — and they can't either — not now. . . . All this senseless, terrible pride —"

"Best you get away from here," Ben said, breaking into her distraught words. "I don't want you anywhere near. . . . You said they were coming — when?"

Marcie had regained her composure somewhat. She glanced over her shoulder to the basin, now slowly clearing itself of dust, then to the broad plains beyond.

"I don't know. I was afraid they might even get here ahead of me. But they're picking up others — ranchers. They're all coming."

Apparently Pete Amber had something in mind other than sudden and violent retaliation. He could be reacting as Ben had suspected and hoped, planning to proceed with caution. Taking the girl by the arm, he guided her back to her horse.

"Thanks for the warning," he said, "and for worrying about me. Things will work out fine."

He helped her to the saddle. She settled her toes in the stirrups and looked down at him soberly.

"You won't leave?"

Keenlyn shook his head. "You wouldn't want me to. You know that."

"No, I guess not," she answered, taking up the reins. "But if only —"

Whatever she intended to say, she abandoned. Leaning over she kissed him lightly.

"Be careful, Ben — please. You're all I've got or want. Even if you lose everything it won't matter as long as you're safe."

Abruptly she wheeled away and headed down into the basin.

Keenlyn spun to his horse. "Don't want Pete and the others knowing where we've got the herd. They'll go by the ranch first. I'll head them off there. You keep back in the rocks out of sight in case Pete puts somebody to snooping around. I'll be back soon as I'm rid of them."

He rode hard for the Box K, anxious to get there well before Amber and the others arrived. He entered the yard a short time later, satisfaction running through him when he saw no sign of the ranchers. Stabling his horse, he pulled his rifle from the boot and hurried to the house. Casimiro met him at the kitchen door.

"The *muchacha* — she looks for you. I send her —"

"Saw her," Ben said, brushing by the older man. "Going to have callers again. The whole bunch. Get me Aaron's shotgun — it's in the bunkhouse."

Casimiro moved off hurriedly, and Keenlyn, passing through the house to the front porch, made a quick study of the forward wall of the building. There were windows at each end.

Returning inside, he walked hastily to the room at the extreme south end of the hall, where he raised the window a few inches. Propping the rifle with a chair back, he wedged the weapon into the opening so that a foot or so of the barrel, aimed toward the hitchrack, was visible.

Casimiro reappeared at that moment with Aaron Cash's old ten-gauge scattergun, and moving to the opposite end of the house, he followed a like procedure. He returned then to the yard and surveyed the arrangement critically. From the outside it looked as if two guns ably covered any who drew to a halt at the rail.

Valdez watched him in silence, and when Ben, satisfied, reentered the house, he said, "There will be trouble, eh?"

"Maybe," Keenlyn said, checking his pistol. "I want you to stay in the kitchen. Be safe there."

Casimiro drew himself erect. "I have a *pistola,* señor. I will stand by your side."

Ben put his arm around the older man's thin shoulders. "Thanks, *amigo.* I'm obliged to you, but there's no sense your getting hurt if things blow up."

"In my country I was thought to be very good with a *pistola.*"

Keenlyn looked more closely at Valdez. He was sincere in his offer to help. He would feel slighted if refused — and he, too, had pride.

"I shall be honored to have you with me," he said in Spanish, and then, in English, added, "Get your pistol, wear it where it can be seen. Like you to stand in the doorway while I'm talking to them."

Casimiro bobbed his head soberly. "I understand. Aaron and Chet — they will come?"

"No. They've got to stay with the cattle. Be just you and me — and those two guns sticking out of the windows."

The aged Mexican smiled. "We fool them, señor. There is a saying in my country that

70

the little fox always outsmarts the fierce tiger."

As the Mexican moved off, Ben threw his glance toward the road. . . . No one in sight.

Casimiro returned, a rusting long barreled old cap-and-ball pistol thrust into the waistband of his cotton trousers. The Mexican patted the ornate butt proudly and sat down in a chair in a corner of the room.

Time wore on. . . . Casimiro retired to the kitchen, returned later with cups of coffee, bread and meat, slices of pie. Keenlyn ate, became restless. Where the hell were they? Were they coming or not? He glanced at the thick German-silver watch that had been his father's. . . . Almost four. . . . What was keeping them?

"Señor . . ." Valdez said, and pointed through the open doorway.

Ben crossed the room in a long stride. There were riders at the far end of the road — a dozen, at least. Pete Amber had brought plenty of company.

XII

Keenlyn waited until the cavalcade had filed into the yard fronting the house, and then he stepped out onto the porch. Arms folded, he moved to the edge of the weathered boards, halted, coolly touched each man with his glance.

Besides Pete and Jack Amber and the everpresent Gabe Carlin, there were Ragland, Suber, Fritz Kemmer, along with Town Marshal Melrose, livery stable owner Carl Linderman, Joe Hoffman, who ran the feed store, and several others who lived in town. Noticeable by their absence were Gorman Hensley and Sol Seligman.

Ben greeted the men with a curt nod as they drew up in front of the rack. Facing Pete Amber, he asked, "What's this all about?"

"The marshal'll do the talking," the rancher said, settling back in his saddle.

Faint surprise rippled through Keenlyn as he shifted his attention to the old lawman. From the tail of his eye he saw several of the riders taking in the guns leveled at them from the windows.

"What's on your mind, Marshal?"

Melrose cleared his throat, nervously

glanced to Pete Amber, then said, "Serious charges here, Ben. Destroying private property . . . arson . . ."

Keenlyn's brows lifted. "Arson?"

"Pete Amber claims you raided his place last night and burned down a corral and several buildings. Endangered lives. Mighty serious."

Ben was only half-listening. His gaze was on Pete Amber. The sheer brass of the man was hard to believe! The utter gall — charging him with arson, with destroying property!

"You've got the guts of a mule!" he exploded. "You set fire to my range, slaughter fifty head of my stock, cause the death of one of my crew — and then come here with the law trying to arrest me for arson!"

The rancher met his furious anger coolly. "You admitting to it?"

Ben caught hold of his temper. "You admit setting fire to my range first, killing my beef — murder?"

Melrose half-turned and looked at the men lined up behind him. "Murder?"

"Buck Grimmer," Keenlyn said. "Was caught in the stampede Amber's bunch started. Far as I'm concerned it was murder." He paused. Then, "Hold it, Jack," he said as the younger Amber and Gabe Carlin began to drift slowly toward the end of the house.

The two men halted. Jack said, "Why?" in a sly sort of voice.

"Could be you'll find some guns back there, too."

Carlin's eyes opened wider. "You bring in some help?"

"Finding out could be unhealthy," Keenlyn said quietly. "Smartest thing you can do is stay out here in front where I can see you."

Jack glanced to Carlin and shrugged, and then both came around slowly and resumed their places at the end of the hitchrack.

"You say Buck was caught in a stampede?" Suber asked, apparently sober for a change.

Ben nodded. "Happened the way I told it. You know anything about firing my grass, slaughtering my beef, Ed?"

Suber looked down, shook his head.

Keenlyn shifted his eyes to Ragland and Kemmer. "Either one of you?"

Both men made their denial, Homer Ragland by a shake of his head, Kemmer by a weak "No."

Ben came back to Amber. "Leaves paying the bill up to you, Pete. Owe me for fifty steers. Twenty dollars a head — comes to a thousand. Grass'll be something else. Be up to the marshal what he wants done about Buck."

Pete Amber's face had become a glowing

red flag under his wide-brimmed hat. He stirred angrily. "This ain't what we come here for — all this damn talking!" He turned to the old lawman. "All right, Floyd — what're you holding back for?"

Melrose mopped at his lined face helplessly. "But he's claiming you done the same to him — caused one of his men to get killed. I — I hardly —"

"You're right, Marshal," Keenlyn snapped. "Not much of anything you can do unless you want to take him in on the same charges — maybe a few more."

"You resisting arrest — defying the law. That it?" Linderman said then.

"No more than Pete Amber is," Ben replied evenly.

"Charges been brought against you, not him. And if you refuse to go in with Melrose, that's what you'll be doing."

"Then that's what I'm doing, because I'm not getting tricked into a deal Pete's cooked up," Ben said, and turned back to Melrose. "Seems to me, Marshal, best thing for you is to keep out of this. They're using you — that's all. They don't give a goddamn about the law. Just trying to make things look good."

"Now, wait a minute —"

But Ben cut the marshal off.

"Expect there's a few more people in this

county who won't exactly go along with Pete's high-handed way of doing things. And there's other law outside Ute Springs, too — the U. S. Marshal's office, for one thing."

Jack Amber spurred forward angrily. "You try calling in the U. S. Marshal —"

Pete waved him back. "Don't get all riled up. He won't. Happens the seat of his pants is black as mine. Few things he'd not want to try explaining."

"Tell my side of it any time you're ready to tell yours," Keenlyn said.

"This could all be settled easy," Ragland said, shifting on his saddle. "Good chance we can get Hensley's people to double their offer. You take it, Ben, and this kind of thing is done with."

Keenlyn was shaking his head even before the rancher had finished speaking. "No dice. Place is not for sale."

Jack Amber swore harshly and again made a threatening move forward. Ben eyed him sharply.

"Getting fed up with you, mister. Try that once more and you could end up with a belly full of buckshot."

"Maybe — but you'd be dead too. Gabe and the others'd cut you down so quick —"

"So I'd be dead — along with you and your pa — because I'd get him first and some of

76

the rest. That scattergun's not the only thing looking down your throats."

"It and one rifle — that's all I see. I got a hunch you're bluffing, and I —"

"Settle down, Jack," Pete Amber broke in irritably. "That mouth of yours does too damned much flapping."

Pete leaned forward, eyes boring into Keenlyn. "What's making you so hard-nosed about this?" he demanded. "You just taking pleasure in bucking me?"

"Long way from that," Ben replied with a sigh. "Buried a good man today because he felt the same as I do. But you wouldn't understand that kind of feeling, Pete. A piece of land is just so much dirt to you. It's not that way with everybody. But like I said, you'd not understand, and there's no way of making you. Now if you're done, ride on. And don't come back."

"You threatening me?"

"Take it any way you like. Point is, I catch anybody from Seven Bar inside my lines from here on, I wont promise he'll ride out."

"Reckon that's plain enough. Same goes for you. Far as you and your bunch is concerned, Seven Bar is closed range."

"Seems that's settled," Linderman observed dryly. "What about the charges that's been brought. You refusing to let the marshal —"

"The marshal knows what he can do with those charges," Keenlyn said with a humorless smile. "So does Pete."

The stableman shrugged and turned away as the others began to move off. "So be it," he said. "Reckon you know what you're doing."

XIII

Ben Keenlyn watched in thoughtful silence as the party rode off. He'd been lucky. He'd been able to turn Pete Amber's own words against him. And those damned fool charges Pete had trumped up — a joke, and he'd made them all see it. All but Carl Linderman. He couldn't quite figure the livery stable owner.

It had been easy — too easy, he thought, as small doubts began to creep into his mind. It wasn't like Pete Amber to back off so readily. Was the whole thing a carefully worked-out scheme to put him in an indefensible position?

The ridiculous charges, the presence of Floyd Melrose, representing the law, the several persons from town — able witnesses who could testify if need be that he had refused to submit to arrest. He understood now what Linderman's final words meant — he had made of himself an outlaw.

Ben swore silently. He had walked right into Pete Amber's trap. He had played his hand just exactly the way the rancher had hoped he would. The next move wasn't hard to figure. Melrose, old and ineffectual, would need help to enforce his law. Amber would be right there offering a half dozen good men as deputies to assist in bringing in an outlaw. Somewhere along the way the outlaw would attempt an escape — and he wouldn't make it . . .

But why would Pete go to all the trouble? He had never before gone to any pains where the law or the opinions of others were concerned. . . . Hensley — that was the answer. The land agent had evidently made it plain to Amber he'd stand for no bloodshed, no violence that might lead to later problems. . . .

Ben shrugged tiredly, pivoted, and entered the house. Casimiro greeted him with a wide grin.

"We fool them, no?"

"Fooled somebody — maybe ourselves," Keenlyn muttered.

The old cook frowned. "What is it you say, señor?"

"Could be I outsmarted myself."

He halted in the center of the kitchen assembling his thoughts. He could ride to the Territorial Capital, look up the U. S. Marshal, lay his problem before him. But the government, unlike Melrose, would want substantiated proof.

That some sort of move would be made against him was inevitable — either one led by Pete Amber or at least one inspired by him with Floyd Melrose fronting. The question was when. Pete would be smart enough not to push hard; he'd wait a day, perhaps two. That was good. Ben would have a chance to mull things over, come up with something. He just might go see the U. S. Marshal, after all.

"Get a little grub together," he said, turning to Casimiro. "Enough for two men, couple of days."

"We are camp in the hills?"

"Won't be necessary for all of us to. I don't think they'll hit the house now, but I am aiming to keep the herd out of sight until this thing clears up."

Two hours later Keenlyn was back in the box canyon. Aaron Cash had elected to stay the night with Ben and the cattle, allowing Chet Buntin, in rough shape after the backbreaking labor he'd withstood for two days and a night, to return to the ranch and the comfort of a good bed.

"Sure sounds like a put-up job," the old puncher said when Keenlyn had related the encounter with Amber and the others.

Ben stared off toward the Saddlebows to the west, where the sun was dropping swiftly out of sight in a brilliant spray of orange. "Way it stands, they've jockeyed me into a pretty tight corner."

"Ain't no arguing that," Aaron said with

a yawn. "And folks'll forget it was Pete and his bunch that opened the ball."

Keenlyn reached for his cup, poured himself a fresh measure of coffee. Cash and Chet had prepared a fairly comfortable camp behind a jutting shoulder of rock just within the mouth of the canyon.

"Herd give you any trouble?" he asked as Aaron sprawled out on his bedroll.

"Nothing much so far, but I expect tomorrow'll be different. Going to start bawling for water before long. How long we going to keep them here?"

Ben shook his head. "Wish I knew. Guess the answer to that lays in what Pete Amber does next." He glanced again to the mountains in the west. The last of the sun's glare was gone.

"I'll take the first watch," he continued. "Gets to where I can't keep my eyes open, I'll wake you."

The old puncher yawned, stretched once more. "Seems I ain't had no shut-eye for a month of Sundays. Figure you can keep awake?"

Ben took another swallow of the strong, black coffee. "I'll manage."

Aaron rolled into his blanket. "Now, you be dang sure you get me up. Don't you go setting there all night."

It wasn't likely, Keenlyn thought. His eyes were already heavy, and the coffee was proving of little benefit. Putting the cup on a nearby ledge, he rose, took up his rifle, and moved quietly out of the pocket to the mouth of the canyon.

The night, silvered by a three-quarter moon, lay hushed and warm. A coyote barked from the ridges of the Feathers, got his reply from somewhere out on the flats. It was a beautiful, serene land; it was hard to believe that with the coming of the sun, it could very possibly change into a harsh world of violence and spilled blood.

Wheeling, he doubled back up the canyon for a look at the herd. All was quiet there too. The stock had bedded down, lulled by the night, but that, also, could change. He couldn't hope to keep them penned up indefinitely. The need for water would turn them unmanageable.

Then what?

It was a question he couldn't answer. Who could possibly guess what Pete Amber had in mind? He would strike, yes — but where? How?

Ben Keenlyn stirred wearily. He'd take it an hour at a time — meet each hour with whatever was necessary.

XIV

Keenlyn awakened to find Aaron Cash bending over him shaking his shoulder. It was long past dawn. He sat up suddenly.

"Rider coming," the old puncher said.

Ben sprang to his feet and crossed to the edge of the rocks, where he could look out onto the flat.

"Having hell staying on the saddle," Aaron commented, shading his eyes and squinting. "Say — ain't that your buckskin?"

"It is," Keenlyn said. "And Chet's riding him. Something's wrong."

Both men hurried down to the mouth of the canyon, now filled with the restless grumbling of the irritable cattle. Buntin drew nearer, a hunched shape on the buckskin, head slung low, both hands gripping the saddle horn.

"Been hurt, sure as hell," Aaron muttered. "That goddamn Pete Amber — he —"

Keenlyn rushed forward. In a moment Ben had the reins in hand and was leading the horse back into the canyon. Cash met him, lifted the near-unconscious man from the saddle and lowered him to his bedroll.

"Been shot twice," he said, probing under

the wounded man's bloodstained shirt.

Ben knelt over Buntin. The wounds were in his chest — and bad. Anger kindling quickly within him, he peered closer at the man.

"Chet — what happened?"

Chet coughed deeply, brushed weakly at his lips. Aaron rose, crossed to his saddlebags, and returned with a half-full bottle of whiskey.

"Have yourself a swallow of this here lightning," he said, holding the liquor to Chet's mouth.

Buntin gulped a drink, sighed and settled back. He focused his eyes on Ben. "Was Jack — Jack Amber . . . and a bunch from Seven Bar. . . . Hunting you. . . . Claim you drygulched Pete."

Keenlyn stiffened with surprise. "Pete Amber's dead?"

"Found him . . . 'round midnight. Up there on your range . . . where the road cuts across the corner."

"Why me?"

"Said you promised . . . kill him . . . you ever caught him on your land."

Pete Amber dead. It was hard to believe — and it made no sense, did not fit the picture. Pete certainly would not have arranged his own death just to strike back.

"Gates of hell are sure open now," Aaron

muttered, brushing at his eyes.

"Casimiro — he's dead . . . too," Buntin said.

"Old Cass?" Aaron exclaimed, giving way to anger. "Why them lousy, stinking bastards — shooting down a poor old —"

"Tried to stop them . . . setting fire to the house. . . . Walked right out . . . front of them. Had a old cap-and-ball hogleg. . . . Somebody . . . don't know who . . . shot him."

Keenlyn swore bitterly. First Buck Grimmer, now Casimiro. And likely Chet Buntin was living the last minutes of his life.

"Was then . . . I got loose . . . run for it. . . . They winged me . . . leaving. . . . Had to get here . . . time to warn . . . you." Chet paused, swallowed with difficulty. He fixed his glazing eyes on Ben. "You . . . got to pull out. After you now. . . . Can't fight . . . dozen men."

Hate — cold, hard, and throbbing steadily — gripped Ben. This was the end of it. He'd let it go no farther.

"I'll be waiting for Jack," he said.

Aaron had formed two pads from a clean rag and was stanching the flow from Chet's wounds. He looked up impatiently. "Now, that's damn foolishness! What good would it do? Get yourself killed sure. And they'd walk off scot-free 'cause they'd cut down a killer — all lawful and everything."

Ben's eyes were on the sky to the southeast. An ugly smudge was pinned against the horizon. The ranch was going up in flames. Jack and his crowd would be coming soon. The man who'd shot Buntin would have marked the direction he'd taken.

"Smart thing for you to do is get out of here, hole up. You're wanted for murder now, boy. Let things cool off a mite, then start looking for who really done it."

Aaron's words made sense. Someone had killed Pete Amber for the specific purpose of throwing the blame upon his shoulders, to get him out of the way. Even if he wanted to leave Bloodrock Valley and find a new life elsewhere with Marcie Ragland, it was now impossible. No man could live in peace under the threat of a murder warrant.

He looked down at Chet Buntin. The cowhand was resting easier.

"Who found Pete?"

Chet stirred. "Nobody said. . . . Listen to Aaron, boy. . . . Don't try . . . fighting them." Buntin began to cough again. Aaron Cash waited until the spasm passed, then held the bottle to the man's bloodless lips and induced him to take another long swallow.

Keenlyn nodded. He guessed it would be

senseless to remain there. Such could only result in his getting killed along with Aaron.

"Was the marshal with them?"

Chet moved his head slowly. "Was only Jack and Carlin — a bunch of . . . Seven Bar . . . hardcases."

Ben walked to the outthrust of rock and stared across the flat. Immediately his eyes picked up a boil of dust far to the south. That would be Jack Amber and his party, following the trail left by Chet. It would bring them straight to the canyon.

He turned and trotted to his horse. Jamming his rifle into the boot, he probed in the saddlebags for extra cartridges. Taking up the reins, he swung back to where Aaron still crouched over Buntin. Chet's features were slack, his skin a bleached gray. Aaron caught Ben's eye and shook his head.

A wild fury again rocked Keenlyn, but he choked it back. Hunching beside the dying man he took his hand into his own.

"Obliged to you, Chet, for — for everything. I'm doing what you say, riding on. Aim to keep them away from here so you won't be bothered."

"Reckon . . . they won't bother me — not . . . for long. Aaron, here . . . howsomever . . . he . . ."

His voice trailed off into nothing. Cash got

to his feet, his long frame trembling. "Another good man we owe them goddamn bastards for," he said, grinding out the words. "I'm going with you. We'll get back in the hills, pick them sidewinders off one by one when they show up."

Keenlyn was the cool one now. "No," he said. "We'll do like you and Chet wanted. Trying to fight them is what Jack's hoping for. We'd not last long. We'll make him play this game our way."

"How?"

"I'll let them see me, draw them off. Can lose them in the Feathers easy. You stay with the herd — hold it here in the canyon long as you can."

"Ain't going to be easy. Reckon I could throw a brush fence across the mouth of the canyon."

"Good idea, only be sure nobody sees you working at it. Got enough grub to last a couple of days?"

"Can manage. When'll you be back?"

"Soon as I shake Jack and his bunch, I'll start nosing around, see what I can find out about Pete's killing. Have to do it soon, before the trail gets cold."

"Everybody's going to be on the lookout for you. Best go mighty careful."

"I will. You hold out here long as possible.

It gets to where you can't, turn the herd loose. We can round the stock up later — if there's any need."

Aaron Cash nodded his understanding. "It comes to that, don't reckon it'll matter much to either one of us. . . . *Adiós,* son — and good luck."

"Same to you," Ben said, grasping the older man's outstretched hand.

Wheeling, he stepped to the saddle and headed for the mouth of the canyon.

XV

The smoke rising from the burning structures of the Box K formed a huge dirty-gray pall in the southeast. There'd be nothing left standing. Jack Amber would make a thorough job of it.

He'd owe Jack for that — and for Casimiro Valdez and Chet Buntin — especially for the aged Mexican. There'd been no need for shooting him down. He was old, harmless. It was doubtful whether the ancient weapon he had brandished would even fire.

It was different where Chet Buntin and men like him were concerned. They were experienced both in the use of a weapon and in facing the likes of Jack Amber and those who rode with him. But poor, loyal old Casimiro . . .

The corners of Keenlyn's jaw hardened. The deaths of all three men had been so useless — so unnecessary! Grimmer because he was only doing his job; Chet Buntin and Casimiro because of a mistake — because Jack Amber had jumped to a conclusion and taken it upon himself to avenge the murder of his father.

Maybe Ben did appear to be the logical killer, but Jack should have at least tried to make sure. But that wasn't the Amber way of doing things. Pete had always moved in a high-handed manner, never doubting his own thoughts and decisions; Jack was just like him.

Ben reached the mouth of the canyon and halted. The dust cloud was still well to the south, and that was to his liking. He wanted to be a considerable distance from the box where the herd was hidden when Jack and the others saw him. The farther from that point he could keep Amber, the better.

Cutting sharp left, he rode along the edge of the foothills and low bluffs for a good mile and then began to swing away at right angle, pointing west. Shortly, he was clear of the hills and on the open flat and again he pulled to a stop.

The roll of dust was much nearer. They should be spotting him, he thought, and then drew to abrupt attention. A second group of riders was cutting in from the rough country to the east. Jack had split his party, sent half to search out the brushy, rock-studded area below the canyon.

He grinned tightly. He had swung away from the hills just in time. Ten minutes later and they would have seen him riding away from the box where Aaron Cash was holding the herd. He spurred forward, heading directly toward the approaching riders. Best to make it appear he was coming in from the range and knew nothing of what had taken place at the ranch.

The knot of riders who had been scouring the brakes swerved suddenly and hurried to rejoin the main party. They had seen him. He pulled the bay to a slow walk, eyes on the men. They merged, hesitated briefly, and then all surged forward as a single unit, horses at a fast gallop.

Immediately Keenlyn cut about and, digging spurs into the tough little gelding, drove straight across the flat on a due-north course.

Two or three gunshots flatted across the warm air, faint and wavering, a sheer waste of effort and gunpowder. The distance that separated them was so great that he could not distinguish any of the riders, not even Jack Amber himself. But the shots were an indication of the mood the party was in and proof positive of what they had in store for him.

The bay held his own with no effort. They drew abreast of the box canyon, so distant to his right that he could neither hear nor see any sign of the old puncher and the cattle. He looked then to the ragged, rocky slopes of the Feathers.

He'd best start angling toward the towering mass soon. He'd not make the mistake of trying to outrun Amber's party for an indefinite time. There'd be two or three fast horses in the pack that, over several miles, could probably close the gap and bring him within rifle range. The bay, built more for endurance than for speed, would do better in the mountains.

Well past the canyon, Keenlyn began to curve east, striking for a small valley that led into the wild fastness of the mountains. It was familiar country. He'd grown up in the area and spent countless hours as a boy roaming the Feathers, seeking out the deep canyons, prowling the ridges, crossing the grass-covered saddles that swung gracefully from peak to peak.

His eyes caught motion ahead and to his left. Riders — a half dozen or so. They popped into view from behind a roll of land — coming from the north. He felt his nerves tighten. More of Jack Amber's Seven Bar crowd. Apparently they had not been on hand when the raiders left the Amber ranch but were now cutting across country to join the party.

Suddenly the advantage was no longer his. He was caught between the two groups, both closing fast. He'd have to reach the protection of the Feathers — and do so quickly.

The newcomers judged the situation correctly and opened up, their yells riding above the flat, hollow crackle of their pistols.

Amber's main party, encouraged by their appearance, began to use their weapons also, goading their mounts to an even faster pace.

Grim, Ben Keenlyn crouched low over the bay, pressing him for every ounce of speed. The distance was still too great for effective shooting, but someone with a rifle could get lucky and hit him or the horse. And he was still a full mile from the foot of the mountains. He'd barely make it — if the breaks were with him.

He threw a glance over his shoulder to the larger party. He recognized Jack, out a stride in the lead, mercilessly flogging the big sorrel he forked. The riders who had come in from the north were nearer, and Jack appeared to be striving to overcome their lead, determined to be first in for the kill.

Only there'd be no kill — not if he could reach the rocks and brush, Ben thought. He put his attention ahead. The first outcropping was less than a hundred yards distant. The gelding was straining hard, every muscle of his compact body taut. Sweat was beginning to lay dark patches on his hide, and the whites of his eyes were showing. He couldn't stand the pace much longer.

Ben reached down, patted the horse's outstretched neck. "Only a little farther," he murmured.

The shooting tempo increased, and once he heard a bullet sing off a nearby rock, but the others fell short or else went wide. He had no great fear of being hit — not just yet, anyway. Later, when the climb into the mountains began and the bay was compelled to slow because of the steep grade, danger would come. But that was when he'd call upon his knowledge of the Feathers' multitude of canyons and numberless ridges for safety.

Suddenly they reached the rocks and the bay was plunging into the sloping entrance of a small wash. Instantly Keenlyn swerved hard left, driving for the trail he knew led through massive piles of boulders accumulated at the foot of a long slope.

The bay began to slow as the footing turned uncertain. Ben looked back. This was the moment he had feared, the time when Amber and the others swept into the wash and he, forced to almost a walk as the gelding began the steep climb, hung pinned against the slope.

His lead had been better than he thought. The bay made the initial stretch in the open and rounded the first bend in the trail, placing a huge shoulder of rock between him and the ground below just as Amber thundered into the wash.

But they had their fleeting glimpse of him. Instantly yells went up. A flurry of gunshots echoed noisily, and bullets splatted against the bulge of granite.

Keenlyn grinned and urged the tiring bay up the trail. He was in the driver's seat again. Now he'd call the turns.

He pressed on, hearing the clatter of pursuit at the foot of the slope — shouts, curses, spilling gravel. Ahead of him the path split. Unhesitating, he swung to the right, taking a narrow trail that followed along the rim of a steadily widening canyon.

Again the path forked. He continued on the right flare for a short distance, then, cutting the gelding about, jumped him over an embankment of loose rock and brush and rejoined the left wing of the trail. Spurring the flagging horse, he moved on a dozen yards and then, in the depths of a dense piñon thicket, halted.

Almost immediately he saw Jack break into view a short distance below. In single file the remainder of the party followed, faces intent, pistols and rifles ready in their hands.

Amber came to the split in the trail, studied the ground briefly, and veered to the right. Moments later he reached the second fork. Again he looked for the telltale hoofprints and followed them.

"This way," he shouted over his shoulder. "He's heading down into the canyon."

From the pungent depths of the piñons, Ben

97

watched the riders move on. Jack wouldn't bother to examine the trail again for tracks unless he encountered another fork, and there'd be none. The path stayed with the rim of the canyon, ending eventually against the sheer face of a butte on the far side where it dwindled into a game trail usable only by deer and other wild animals.

When the last of the Seven Bar men had dropped from sight, Keenlyn pulled out of the thicket and guided the gelding onto the secondary route. Then, keeping the still heaving animal to an easy walk, he began the slow upward journey to the topmost ridge of the Feathers.

It would be a long pull to the crest and down the opposite side to the plains. He'd have plenty of time to think, and perhaps when he reached the flats, he'd have some idea, some plan of what he should do next. Only one thing was crystal-clear in his mind — he had to find Pete Amber's killer.

XVI

It was late afternoon when Ben Keenlyn reached the foot of the Feathers' eastern slope. The day had been long and hard on both him and the bay, and coming finally to level ground, he swung in under a small cottonwood to rest.

He'd go first to Ragland's, he'd decided, and see Marcie. From her he could learn the details of Pete Amber's death. Then he'd have a starting point. It would be necessary to hold off, however, until the rancher had turned in for the night. Ragland, like everyone else in the valley and the settlement, assuming him guilty, would be no friend.

There was time to spare, and he spent a full hour in the shade of the tree, taking his ease and allowing the bay to cool and recover. Ragland's place was just around the end of the mountain, little more than ten miles away. It wouldn't take long to get there.

When the last of the sun was gone he mounted, and keeping close to the foot of the rambling hills, he headed north. He had little fear of being seen by Jack Amber and his party. They would long since have discovered that they'd been led into a blind alley, and they'd have turned back, probably to search the west slopes of the Feathers.

Darkness would have brought that to a halt, since the uncertain, treacherous grades were no place for a horse at night. Likely all were on their way back to Seven Bar by that hour.

The danger came from being noted by others. The road from Ute Springs, cutting its path northward to Colorado and eastward to Dallas and various points elsewhere in Texas, lay but a short distance from the hills. Travelers pursuing its dusty course could see him if they, having been warned, were searching.

He had no idea, of course, whether posses other than Jack Amber's were combing the country for him, but word of the killing would spread fast, and chances were good that they were. It would be wise to play it safe.

It was full dark when he halted in the trees bordering the creek at the edge of Ragland's yard. Lamplight still glowed in the windows of the main house, and there was someone working in the barn. Marcie's room appeared dark, however, and he guessed she had already retired. Sighing, stiff from so many hours in the saddle, he dismounted and found a place to sit on a nearby log. There was nothing to do but wait until all lights were gone.

A short time later the barn darkened and foreman George Rusk came through the doorway, crossed the yard, and entered the small cabinlike structure reserved for him. A yellow glow tinted the small window briefly, then winked out. Only the main house now remained. Finally it, too, went black.

Turned restless by the irritating delay, Keenlyn rose, prowled about in the screening brush for another quarter hour, then mounted and rode quietly in among the buildings, keeping to the shadows as much as possible and halting when he reached the rear of the ranch house. Leaving the bay standing in the darkness near a corral, he crossed to Marcie's window and tapped lightly on the pane.

She was up instantly, peering through the glass. He motioned with his hands, and she raised the sash quietly.

"Ben — I've been so worried!"

He stilled her with a finger against her lips. "Put something on," he said in a low voice. "Got to talk."

She disappeared and returned a moment later, a quilted robe about her slim body. He reached in, caught her around the waist, and lifted her through the opening.

"Over here," he said, putting her down, and drew her into the blackness at the end of the house.

"I knew you'd come," she said at once. "But

I've been so afraid. They're looking for you everywhere."

He nodded. "Had Jack and his bunch on my trail this morning. Shook them in the mountains." He paused, feeling her eyes boring into him, his mind reading her unspoken question. "No, I didn't kill Pete. Never saw him after he left my place late yesterday."

Marcie sighed thankfully. "Did you threaten him — like Uncle Homer said?"

"Probably. I was pretty riled up, and a man says a lot of things at a time like that. Usually too much. But Grimmer'd been killed because of Pete, and I'd lost a lot of beef."

She trembled, and he put his arm around her and held her close.

"This morning Jack and a couple of dozen of his crowd hit my place," he said. "Burned it to the ground. Killed Chet Buntin and Casimiro."

Marcie drew back in horror. "Casimiro — and Chet! Why?"

He shrugged "They worked for me. In a war like this any man on the other side is the enemy. No need for it — especially Casimiro. He never hurt anybody."

The girl lowered her head. "And it will get worse. They'll not stop now until they've found you and shot you down too. They think you're a murderer. The whole valley and everyone in town will keep hunting until finally someone —"

He silenced her again. "Reason I took a chance and came here. Got to know a few things about what I'm supposed to have done if I aim to find the real bushwhacker."

"You don't know?"

"How could I? Aaron and I have been busy with the herd. Drove them into that box canyon at the south end of the mountains, where they'd be safe if Amber's crew tried another raid. First I knew of it was when Chet rode in, half-dead, and told me Pete had been shot and I was supposed to be the one who did it. Who found Pete?"

"Mr. Hensley, the land agent."

Something stirred in Ben Keenlyn's mind. Gorman Hensley had seemed a straight and honorable man, but when you came right down to brass tacks, he probably stood to gain most of all by the sale of the valley. Hensley wouldn't be the first man he'd misjudged.

"Know any details?"

"Only what Uncle Homer told us. Seems Pete Amber had an appointment in town last night with Mr. Hensley. When Pete didn't show up, Hensley rented a horse and started for Seven Bar. He found Pete dead on that strip of the road that cuts across the corner of your range."

"What time? Did Homer mention it?"

"I think he said it was around ten o'clock."

"Doesn't matter too much, I guess. Where was Jack during all this?"

"In town somewhere with Gabe Carlin and some others."

"Probably at Tiffany's. Usually hangs out there. Could find out for sure — if I wanted to risk going in and asking Tiffany."

"You think Jack could have done it?"

"Hated his pa, that's for sure — but he's not alone there. And Hensley — he had good reason. . . . About the only people I'm sure didn't do it are you, me, and Aaron."

She was quiet for a time. Then she asked, "What are you going to do? It all seems so hopeless. . . ."

Keenlyn stirred wearily. "Only way I can save my neck is find who did kill Pete. Going to be quite a chore. . . . Anybody using that old line shack down by your southeast marker?"

"No, not any more. Why?"

"Got to do some figuring and get some sleep. No point in riding all the way back to my place — nothing there. Thought I might spend the rest of the night in that shack and get busy in the morning."

She nodded. "I'll fix some food."

"Won't need it — and you could wake up

somebody in the house."

Taking her by the hand, Ben led her back to the window and lifted her through. She leaned forward and kissed him.

"Don't take any chances, Ben — please."

"I won't. And you stay close to here. County's going to be like a powder keg for a while — don't want you getting hurt. . . . Good night."

"Good night," Marcie murmured as he faded off into the darkness.

Emerald Ragland drew deeper into the shadows of the doorway in which she stood and watched Ben Keenlyn ride quietly out of the yard. Earlier, she had been sitting at the parlor window in the dark, when she saw him come into the place.

At first she wasn't certain it was Keenlyn. It was a bold thing for him to do — ride right up to the ranch, even though night had fallen, when half the county was out looking for him. But Ben Keenlyn was that kind of a man — too much man for Marcie, really.

It was a shame that she must do the chore pure luck had placed in her hands. But Keenlyn was the key, the stumbling block that was preventing her from returning to the city, where she belonged. She'd had all the deadly-silent nights, the vast emptiness with its withering heat, the smell of sweat and manure, that she could take. It was too bad, but it had to be done. And although it pained her to think of such a man going to waste, she'd lose no sleep over it.

It had taken a lot of constant hammering to bring Homer around to seeing things her way, but she was an old hand at persuading men. Actually, she'd thought everything was all set when she maneuvered Homer into accepting the offer Gorman Hensley made for the ranch. She'd begun to make plans, think about the fine time she'd have once they were back in Kansas City or St. Louis, or maybe New York. With all the money they'd have from the sale, they could even make a boat trip to Europe and mix with the high-toned swells.

And then Ben Keenlyn had got bull headed about the deal. Well, Ben Keenlyn wasn't going to queer it for little Emerald. She'd get what she wanted, no matter what it took — and she knew just how to go about it.

Everyone thought Keenlyn had murdered that old windbag of a Pete Amber. They were all out looking for him, Jack most of all. That bit of eavesdropping had afforded her just what she needed — the knowledge of where Keenlyn could be found. That information relayed to Jack Amber — and the problem would be solved.

With Ben Keenlyn out of the way, there'd be nothing to hold up the sale of the ranch to Hensley. Then it was off to all the big towns. *And Homer, old boy, you'd better hang on tight,* she thought, *because little Emerald's been bottled up in the middle of nowhere far too long!*

Stepping softly from the doorway into the yard, she paused and listened intently. The hoofbeats of Keenlyn's horse were fading into silence. Gathering her pink wrapper close, she walked swiftly along the side of the house and made her way to George Rusk's quarters.

Circling the small structure, she rapped sharply three times on the window. Instantly she heard the bed creak, heard his heels hit the floor. George was a useful man. He'd do anything she asked in return for a favor now and then. And he wasn't so bad — big and strong, but stupid.

The door opened, and a moment later he stood beside her. He'd taken time only to pull on his trousers and boots.

"What's the matter?" he asked, his voice faintly hopeful.

She pushed his hands away. "George, I want you to take a message to Jack Amber. It's about Ben Keenlyn."

"Keenlyn?"

"I know where he's hiding."

Rusk was totally silent, and knowing men, she was aware of his thoughts, of the stupid code they insisted on living by. This was none of his business, he was telling himself. He should stay out of it, not be a party to causing the death of another man. Let Jack Amber look after his own problems.

"I want you to ride over to Seven Bar — now. Tell Jack that Keenlyn's sleeping in that old shack in our southeast corner."

Rusk shifted nervously. "I don't know, Emerald —"

"Please, George — for my sake. . . . It's important. After all, he is a murderer. He doesn't deserve any consideration from you or anybody else."

"Maybe Jack'll find him tomorrow anyway."

"And maybe he won't. You've got to let Jack know. And you can tell him, too, that Keenlyn's got his herd hidden in a box canyon somewhere close to his ranch. He'll want to know that. . . . You'd better go along, show him where the shack is."

"He knows where it is."

"All right, but I still want you to go with him, make sure."

"Ain't right. Man oughtn't to mix in where —"

"And then hurry back, George. . . . I'll be waiting."

Rusk straightened in the darkness. "You sure, Emerald? You really will?"

"The sooner you get started, the sooner you'll get back — and find out," she replied, taking him by the arm and pushing him toward the front of the cabin. "Hurry now, George."

He halted, wheeled impulsively, awkwardly planted a kiss on the side of her head, and then trotted off into the darkness.

XVII

The line shack had apparently gone unused for months. There was little doubt that Ragland was neglecting his holdings. Likely, if it weren't for George Rusk the place would go to pot.

The door hung from one hinge, and lifting it to prevent its dragging, he closed it and crossed to one of the two bunks. Dusty blankets covered the hard boards, and taking up one, he shook it gently, not anxious to fill the room with dust. It wouldn't be much of a bed, but it would beat sleeping in the open with no cover at all — and he needed rest.

Stretching out, he stared at the cobwebby ceiling, trying to piece together the scant bits of information he'd gathered and fit them into some sort of picture.

Pete Amber's murder made no sense. Who would want him dead — and why? That the rancher, big and ruthless in his use of power, would have many who disliked him was unquestionable; but who would hate him enough to kill him? Twenty years ago, perhaps, when he was engaged in building his vast Seven Bar spread and thought little of running rough-

shod over anyone who dared oppose him —
yes. But now?

Seemingly, things should be the reverse.
Pete was the man who should be kept alive,
since he was the leader in the popular idea
of selling the valley to Gorman Hensley. All
the ranchers were for it, and so also, it appeared, was everyone in Ute Springs with the
exception of three or four. Why kill the man
who spearheaded the proposal?

He was the thorn in their sides, Ben
thought; he was the solitary opposition. You'd
think he'd be the one in line for murder. With
him dead and out of the way, there'd be no
one left to block Hensley's purchase.

Pete's body had been found on his range,
and the blame for the killing had instantly
been placed on his shoulders. But everyone
used that corner of his range in their traveling
back and forth to town. That it had occurred
there meant nothing.

When Ben had voiced his warning to Pete
Amber and Seven Bar in general to stay off
Box K land, the shortcut route to town had
not entered his thoughts. The strip of ground
had been in public use for so long that he
scarcely considered it his property.

But legally it was — and someone had made
good use of the fact, just as they had marked
well the so-called threat he'd spoken. And

they'd done it for the sole purpose of getting at him.

Who would benefit from Pete's death and his own subsequent elimination because of it? Pete's son, Jack, for one. Jack had long hoped to step into his pa's boots, assume ownership of Seven Bar. With the sale going through he now, as heir, would be the recipient of the large sum of cash from the purchase. If the deal for some reason failed to materialize, he'd still have Seven Bar. Jack was a winner either way — with Pete dead.

And the whole town of Ute Springs, of course, in varying degrees, would profit. The ranchers who wished to sell must be counted in. . . . So also should land agent Gorman Hensley.

Gorman Hensley . . .

He would fare well, and anxious not to lose what would undoubtedly be a large commission for creating and handling the transaction, he would fight anything that jeopardized his possibilities. Further, he had been the one who found Amber's body — late at night and conveniently on the land of a man who'd just threatened the victim a few hours earlier.

Hensley. . . . Ben fought against the heaviness that sought to close his eyes. . . . The land agent was his best bet — his prime suspect. In the morning he'd hunt him up, do a bit of questioning, and see if he could —

Keenlyn sat bolt upright. Somewhere along the way he'd dropped off to sleep, but now he was suddenly and completely awake, some sound or inner sense of danger setting up a warning.

He remained motionless, listening into the darkness of the small hut. Pale streaks of moonlight filtered in around the edge of the poorly fitting door and past the boards nailed over the single window.

Outside the clicking of insects was a continuing murmur, and far back in the Feathers the womanlike scream of a mountain lion etched its unnatural sound across the night. . . . Nothing unusual. Then what —

Keenlyn stiffened. A horse had stamped heavily, blown his wind. Instantly Ben was on his feet and across the room. He placed his eye to the crack between the door and its splintery frame.

Three men. . . . They were moving up to the shack slowly, cautiously, leaving their horses well back in the shadows. Frowning, he studied them closely, unable to determine their identity. Shortly they crossed a strip of open ground where moonlight brought them into definite focus.

Jack Amber, Gabe Carlin, and George Rusk.

That they knew he was inside the line shack

was evident; otherwise, they would not employ such care in their approach. How? No one knew he intended to use the shack — no one, that is, but Marcie Ragland.

Keenlyn felt a coldness sweep through him. He shook it off. Marcie wouldn't have told anyone. Marcie would do nothing to endanger him. There had to be another explanation.

Someone had been eavesdropping, had overheard their conversation in the yard. Rusk, possibly. He then had hurried to get Jack, hoping, no doubt, to make of himself a big man.

A taut grin pulled Keenlyn's mouth into a grim line. They thought they had him cold, trapped in a shack with but one way out. But they could guess again.

Wheeling hurriedly, he jerked the blanket from the second bunk, rolled it with the other, and strung them out full length on the bed directly in front of the door. Bunching the woolen covers to resemble the body of a sleeping man as much as possible, he added his hat, then stepped back for a quick look. In the dark the sham would pass.

Drawing his pistol, he moved to where he would be hidden by the door when it opened.

XVIII

The door opened an inch, caught as it dragged against the rough floor. Jack Amber swore harshly and booted the sagging panel aside. Instantly the room rocked with the deafening crash of two quick gunshots. Smoke and dust boiled toward the ceiling as the figure-shaped blankets jolted from the impact of bullets.

"Takes care of him," Jack said, holstering his weapon as he strode deeper into the shack. Carlin and Rusk, silent, crowded in behind him.

A wild anger ripped through Ben Keenlyn. In that fragment of time he thought of Chet Buntin, of old Casimiro Valdez, of Buck Grimmer — and how it would have been had he not heard Amber and the others. The cold-blooded ruthlessness of Jack Amber was pure animal savagery.

"Don't move!" he snarled, stepping from behind the half-open door.

The men froze. Carlin muttered an oath. Amber and Rusk simply hung motionless, completely silent.

"Get your hands up where I can see them, or goddamn you, I'll blow you through the wall!"

Amber complied instantly. Carlin and Rusk were more deliberate. Keenlyn, fury still gripping him, crossed, removed their pistols one by one, hurled them through the doorway into the brush.

"Turn around!"

They came about slowly. In the pale light streaming into the shack their features were taut, the skin pulled tight over the bones of their faces. Hate glowed in the eyes of Jack Amber, but in the others Ben saw only resignation.

"Get it over with," Carlin said.

Keenlyn considered the three men for a long minute. "What you've got coming," he said finally. "Only I'm not Jack Amber. Better be glad of that."

Carlin murmured something at low breath. Rusk's shoulders went down slowly.

"Nobody'll get hurt," Ben said coldly. "But don't try anything. I'm not that kindhearted."

Amber found his voice. "All right, you've got us. Pull out — no way we can stop you — but don't think it'll end here."

"I'm not going anywhere," Ben said.

Amber's head came forward, a gesture typical of his father. "Then why —"

"Was trying to get a little sleep and stay out of sight until I could figure out who killed your pa and shoved the blame onto me."

"You claiming you didn't do it?"

"I didn't kill him," Keenlyn said, spacing the words distinctly.

"By God, you threatened him — said you'd kill him or any Seven Bar found on your range!"

"Maybe I did, but that's no proof. Far as being on my land, everybody uses that corner. Don't even think of it being mine any more."

Jack shook his head. "Ain't nobody going to swallow that."

"Why the hell would I want to kill him?" Ben snapped impatiently. "We didn't see eye to eye, but I've got nothing to gain with him dead." He paused, looked closely at Jack. "You have."

Amber's head came back sharply. "You saying I done it?"

"I'm saying you had reasons — plenty of them. I've got none. . . . One thing I'd like answered — how'd you know I was here?"

Jack cast an involuntary glance at Rusk, who quickly turned away. "Just heard, that's all."

But Ben had his reply. It was the Arrowhead foreman. Shrugging in disgust, he touched Rusk with his eyes. "You're mighty anxious to be a big man, George."

Rusk shuffled nervously.

"Everybody looks out for Seven Bar,"

117

Amber said, a hint of the old arrogance in his tone.

"It needs looking after," Keenlyn replied dryly. Keeping the men under his gun, he reached down, recovered his hat and backed toward the door.

"Nobody comes outside for ten minutes," he said, halting in the opening. "For what you've done to my crew, to me and my place, I've got every right to shoot you down, and I doubt if anybody'd fault me. . . . Don't press your luck. That clear?"

Amber nodded. The others remained motionless, silent. Keenlyn stepped into the open. Amber's voice checked him. "This mean you're leaving the country?"

"I'll be around — looking for the man who's trying to put a noose around my neck."

Jack shook his head. "There ain't nobody else. Was you. Has to be."

"That kind of thinking has already got you in trouble — with me. I get this cleared up, I'll be looking for you. Owe you for three men. . . ."

"They had guns, wanted to fight."

"Sure — an old cook with a pistol that probably wouldn't even shoot. Another man so tired he could hardly walk, against you and two dozen more. Real brave, Jack, you and your bunch."

"They had no business trying —"

"No point hashing it over now. You did it, and you'll pay for it. . . . Stay put — hear?"

"You ain't getting away with this!" Amber yelled as Keenlyn backed farther into the yard. "That's something you better hear, and hear good. I'll be coming after you!"

"No need," Keenlyn said, stepping into the shadows. "I'll be looking for you."

Immediately he ducked in behind a thick clump of brush and halted to listen. All was quiet for a few moments, and then one of the bunks creaked. Someone sighed gustily. They were settling down, taking him at his word. Pivoting, Ben hurried to where he'd tied the gelding, and pausing only long enough to tighten the slackened cinch, he swung into the saddle and rode off toward the foothills to the east.

Well away from the line shack but at a point where he could watch unseen, he drew to a halt. He was still thinking about George Rusk, puzzling over the man's actions. A dull suspicion was growing within him that more lay behind the foreman's untypical behavior than just a desire for personal acclaim as the one who found the killer of Pete Amber. He'd known Rusk casually for years; he simply wasn't that kind of man.

Could there be someone behind George

Rusk forcing him to act as he did? Did he and that someone have some connection with the murder? It was something to consider.

Jack Amber didn't hold still for the specified ten minutes, as Ben had known he wouldn't. Scarcely half that time had elapsed before a figure appeared in the doorway, hesitated briefly, and then moved into the open. At once Carlin and Rusk emerged, and then all three hurried to the brush fronting the shack, recovered their weapons, and moved on to their horses.

Sleep was no longer in Ben, and there was no point in going in search of Gorman Hensley at that hour of the night. Still disturbed by his thoughts concerning George Rusk and the new possibilities that had developed, he waited until the men had ridden by and then, keeping parallel at a distance, trailed them.

They separated a mile below Ragland's, Jack and Gabe Carlin swinging west for Seven Bar, Rusk riding on until he reached the hardpacked yard behind Arrowhead's ranch house. There he dismounted, led his horse to one of the numerous corrals, and, walking in a quick but quiet fashion, hurried to his cabin.

Emerald Ragland, as if she had been awaiting his arrival, moved from the shadows near the back door of the main building, clad in some sort of pink robe, and crossed quickly to him.

Keenlyn, watching from the darkness alongside the barn, had a moment of embarrassment; he was doing nothing less than spying on what appeared to be a tryst between Homer Ragland's wife and his foreman.

He brushed the feeling of guilt aside. In such he had no interest; a man had been murdered, and he was seeking the killer or clues as to who it might be. His own life depended upon it.

A thought entered his mind. Was it possible that Emerald, in her craving to leave the country and return to city life, had committed the murder through George Rusk?

She could probably persuade the foreman to do anything she wished — but murder? Again he wondered if he really knew George Rusk. There could be a side to the man, warped perhaps by Emerald's breathtaking beauty and honeyed tongue, that Ben was not aware of.

It was food for thought. Turning, he pulled away from the barn and struck south.

He rode on through the pale, early hours that preceded dawn. He could expect to see more of Jack Amber, he knew, but that would come later. Amber would likely gather his crew and begin scouring the country in a systematic search for him after the day began.

Keeping out of his way would be no chore. Ben's next move was to meet with Gorman Hensley. If he could get the man to betray himself, the hunt would be over; if nothing developed there he might at least learn something that would be of help. . . . Getting to Hensley was going to be risky. He was quartering in the hotel in town.

Meanwhile, he had time to spare. He'd have a look at the ranch, the buildings — or what was left of them. And then he'd check on Aaron Cash, see if everything was all right at that point. The old puncher could be in need of something.

He rode into the yard of the Box K an hour later and halted. A combination of despondency and harsh anger stirred him as he looked about. Jack and the men from Seven Bar had done a complete job of it. Nothing was left standing, not even the small tool shed or the peaked canopy over the well. Everything was blackened embers, some still smoking.

All would have to be rebuilt from the ground up. He'd have to start from scratch, and that would take not only time but money — money he'd painstakingly accumulated for the day when Marcie and he could marry. That time was farther in the offing than ever now.

Glum, he moved on until he saw the body of Casimiro Valdez stretched out near what had been the southwest corner of the house. Someone had at least had the decency to throw a scorched blanket over the old man.

Dismounting and locating a spade, he dug another grave alongside that of Buck Grimmer. Using the same blanket, since nothing else was available, he buried the aged Mexican, adding to the unspoken prayer he made over the mound the promise to make Jack Amber pay for what he'd done.

Bitter, the look of his place sickening him, he got back on the bay and struck off toward the canyon where Aaron was holding the herd. Suddenly he had the need for human company, for someone to talk with, someone to help him sort the jumble of thoughts that crowded his mind. He could think of no one better suited to the purpose than Aaron.

XIX

Aaron heard him coming. When Ben emerged from the brush and rode into the mouth of the canyon, the old puncher, rifle poised and ready in his long arms, was standing behind the improvised fence he'd thrown across the entrance. Recognizing Keenlyn, he relaxed and moved to the end of the barrier.

"Bring your horse through here," he said, dragging aside a narrow portion of dry greasewood. "Weren't right sure who I was having for company."

Keenlyn rode into the coulee and dismounted. He peered at Aaron closely, noting the man's haggard features. "Everything all right?"

"Right as you can expect. Cattle's getting mighty spooky. What about you? Have any trouble shaking Jack?"

Ben shook his head and moved to the low fire, where coffee simmered over the coals. Taking up the lard tin, he helped himself to a deep swallow. Then, squatting on his heels, he related the information he had obtained from Marcie.

When he had finished, Aaron scratched at his beard and said, "Sure is a puzzlement. Was

I having to guess, I'd say this here Hensley's at the bottom of it."

"Or it could be Emerald Ragland."

The old puncher's jaw dropped in astonishment. "That wife of Homer's? What makes you think she . . . ?"

"Maybe she didn't pull the trigger," Ben explained, and proceeded to tell Cash of the apparent eavesdropping, by either Rusk or Emerald, and the subsequent encounter in the line shack with Jack Amber, Rusk, and Gabe Carlin.

Aaron stared into the fire. "Beats all. Never figured George'd get down that low, but I reckon a fellow never knows for sure what another'n will do. 'Specially when he's so sot on a woman he can't see from here to there. What're you aiming to do?"

"Giving Rusk the benefit of the doubt — at least for now. Going to look up Hensley, talk to him."

"Ride into town? You can't do that, boy!"

"Manage it somehow."

"You ain't going to have a whole lot of time for doing anything — Jack'll see to that. What if Hensley proves he couldn't have done it?"

"Then George Rusk's next on the list."

"Seems likely — him and that woman of Ragland's."

"And I'm not forgetting Jack himself. Always figured he hated his pa, was looking for the day he could take over Seven Bar."

"Wouldn't put it past him," Aaron said, adding more coffee grounds and water to the lard tin.

"Ed Suber's a good possibility too. Wants to sell bad. And I guess we'd as well include Dutch Kemmer and Ragland too. They were all for the deal, wanted to see it go through."

"Dutch wasn't too anxious — and if you're going to look at it that way, might as well keep right on going, name off all them jaspers in town who're hankering to get rich off all the new business that'd be coming in. Hell, you could say half the people in the county could've bushwhacked Pete and put the blame on you."

"That's what makes it so goddamn hard to figure anything!" Keenlyn said in a sudden burst of irritation. "Every time I start getting the thing sort of squared around in my head, think I'm coming up with an answer, I run into a rock. Everybody had a reason — yet their doing it makes no sense."

Aaron rose, walked to the edge of the brush, and stared off into the basin. First light had not yet broken the darkness, and the moon still held the land in a soft silver haze. After a few moments he wheeled and made his way

126

back to the fire. Ben glanced up at him questioningly.

"Thought I heard something. Some kind of a varmint, I expect. You go by the ranch?"

Ben nodded morosely. "Nothing but ashes. We get through this and figure to start again, it'll mean rebuilding everything."

"Won't be too big of a job," Aaron said, trying to lighten the moment. "Most of them sheds and things was about to fall down anyway." He hesitated, his eyes resting on the blanket-shrouded figure of Chet Buntin. "The little Mex — was he . . . ?"

"Buried him," Keenlyn said. "Next to Buck. When I head for town to see Hensley, I'll take Chet, put him alongside too."

"Sure a hell of a thing," Aaron murmured. "Done some thinking about them. Aim to set up a grave marker for all three. Going to write on it, 'Dead — thanks to the Ambers,' so everybody'll know."

"Seven Bar'll have a few to bury too," Ben said.

The minutes wore on while the sky behind the towering hills to the east pearled gradually and began to show tongues of pink and orange and the buttes, like granite tapestries, slowly took on color. A light wind sprang up from the long plains in the west.

Aaron got to his feet and began to rummage

around in the sack of grub Casimiro had so hastily prepared. "Ain't much left," he said. "Was so danged hungry yesterday I was about three pounds lightern'n a straw hat and et up about everything. Want some dried meat?"

"You go ahead. I'll pass, get mine later. Turns out you have to stay here after today, I'll bring some grub to you."

"Today could just be all I'm staying here whether I want to or not," Cash said, looking up the canyon to where the herd was beginning to stir. "Them critters are turning mighty uneasy. They're thirsting for water, and they know the creek's back down in the basin. This wind, bringing the smell, ain't going to help things none."

Keenlyn glanced to the sky and came upright. "If I have any kind of luck at all with Hensley, we won't have to keep them penned up much longer. Let you know soon as I've had my talk with him."

Aaron abandoned the depleted sack of provisions and followed Ben to his horse. "Sure don't like this here idea of you agoing into town. . . . And that Jack — you can figure on him starting right out first thing hunting you."

"Only way I can talk to Hensley is go see him. Far as Jack's concerned, I'll be on the watch for him. Sooner or later we're going to meet and settle things anyway."

"Know that, but it's got to be when the odds ain't twenty to one."

"I'll pick the time — and the place," Keenlyn said quietly, and swung into the saddle.

Instantly a rifle shot blasted through the early-morning hush. The bullet, brushing Keenlyn's shoulder in its flight, smashed into a rock slide a dozen yards beyond him in the canyon, arousing a chain of echoes and setting up an immediate response among the restless, thirsty cattle.

"Bushwhacker!" Aaron yelled.

Ben was already dropping to the ground, eyes reaching out into the tangle of brush below the entrance to the canyon. Hunched low, he tried to locate the hidden rifleman.

"See him?" Cash asked, moving up beside him.

Keenlyn shook his head. "In that *chamiza* below us somewhere. When it gets lighter, maybe —"

"Ain't going to be no time for that," Aaron said, "look yonder!"

Ben followed the older man's leveled finger. A quarter mile farther away, at the edge of the basin, a score of riders were closing in. Clouds of dust lifted behind them, rolled ahead on the wind. It was not difficult to determine who they were; the man in the center was astride Pete Amber's yellow stallion.

"Jack and his bunch," Aaron muttered. "Dragging in brush. Bastards are aiming to burn us out. Now, how'd they know where we'd holed up?"

Keenlyn remembered. He'd mentioned to Marcie that they'd hidden the cattle in the box canyon, that Aaron was standing watch. Whoever had overheard them — Rusk or Emerald Ragland — had relayed that information to Jack Amber.

"In this danged wind, fire'll come up through here just ahelling," Aaron said, "and there ain't nothing we can do to stop it. Reckon that's why that bushwhacker's there — keeping us pinned down so's we can get roasted."

"Maybe," Ben said. He was having doubts about that. Jack wouldn't have gone to the trouble — he had them trapped anyway. And the man in the brush, whoever he might be, was a considerable distance from the Seven Bar party. . . . No, this was something else — someone on his own out to kill. A stillness settled over Keenlyn. This could be the man who'd tried to drygulch him the night of the raid. . . . This could be the killer of Pete Amber — now out to finish what he had started.

Immediately he drew back from the rocks and, leading his horse well to the side, began to pull down the brush barricade Aaron Cash had erected.

The old puncher frowned. "What're you —"

"Let's get this fence out of the way," Ben snapped. "We'll hand Jack and whoever that is laying out there in the brush a little surprise."

Aaron, still not understanding, began to help. "Just don't see what you're aiming to do."

"We stay put, we lose the herd to fire — and maybe ourselves with it. We'll get the jump on them — and maybe we're going to flush us out a killer at the same time."

XX

The herd was milling nervously by the time the last of the brush fence had been thrown aside. Immediately Ben Keenlyn hurried to his horse and swung into the saddle.

"Get behind them!" he shouted to Cash. "Start them running."

The bushwhacker's rifle cracked again, the sound almost drowned by the bawling of the cattle. The bullet struck somewhere in the rocks. Glancing back, Ben saw that Amber and the others had paused, apparently having heard the gunshot this time.

Spurring the gelding, Keenlyn bulled his way through the fringe of the herd, now shifting toward the mouth of the canyon, and worked his way along the steep slope until he was slightly above the cattle. Across the sea of heaving brown-and-white bodies he could see Aaron Cash in a like position but a bit farther ahead.

"Get them running!" he yelled and, drawing his pistol, fired two quick shots into the back wall of the canyon.

Instantly the herd broke and began to flow toward the basin, the noise of their passage a deafening, echoing din in the confines of the rock-filled box. At once Keenlyn found himself enveloped in a choking haze of dust.

Pulling the bay around, he began to move for the mouth of the canyon, keeping well up on the slope to avoid the now rushing herd. It was tricky going; the footing was uncertain, and if the gelding slipped he'd end up under the pounding hooves of the frantic steers. But by taking it slow he reached the narrow entrance without mishap. The opening was solid across with wildly charging cattle racing to get to the water they could smell on the wind.

"Over there — the bushwhacker!" Aaron's voice, carrying faintly over the thunder of the herd, brought Keenlyn half-around. Following the puncher's pointing finger, he saw through the billowing dust a dim shape running hard for the higher ground to the south. A loose horse was racing off in the opposite direction, fear driving him at top speed.

The dim shape stumbled, fell, bounded upright quickly, and plunged on. Suddenly he was caught in a wedge of steers carrying in from the flank of the herd. He tried to turn, but the horns of a steer raked him, knocking him off-balance. He disappeared briefly, rose to his feet, and then was abruptly gone as a solid wall of cattle swept over him.

Helpless, caught at the mouth of the canyon and unable to break out into the clear, Keenlyn was powerless to do anything except watch. One thing was certain — the man who had sought to kill him was now himself dead or near death.

Ben looked beyond the herd, trying to see what had become of Jack Amber and his crew. Dust hung in a dense cloud above the cattle, and he could make out only a few of the riders, some gathered on one side of the basin, a few on the other. Whether the remainder of Seven Bar men had escaped or been trapped in front of the stampede it was impossible to tell. All would have had time to get in the clear.

The last of the herd was shouldering through the opening. Roweling the bay, Keenlyn dropped off the embankment and met Aaron Cash, coming from the opposing side. The old puncher wiped at the dust settled on his face as he peered through the dry fog.

"Better be hightailing it out of here. Jack and his bunch'll be coming soon's they can get through."

"Got a hunch about that bushwhacker," Ben replied. "Take a look at him first."

"Could be one of Jack's boys too."

"Chance I've got to take," Ben said, heading out into the basin.

He cut diagonally across the edge of the swale, pointing for the crumpled gray shape lying a short distance to his left. Vaguely he could hear shooting over in the direction of the still racing herd. Seven Bar was still fighting to keep the cattle bunched in the center of the basin.

Reaching the trampled man, Ben dropped to the ground. Kneeling, he took the crushed shoulders in his hands and rolled the man to his back. Behind him Aaron Cash swore in startled surprise.

"By God — Ragland! Never figured —"

Keenlyn stared at the rancher's distorted features in disbelief. Homer Ragland opened his eyes slowly. Pain dragged at his lips.

"Don't . . . touch me," he groaned.

Hoofbeats were drumming, growing louder. Ben threw a hurried glance toward the basin. He recognized Gabe Carlin and two other Seven Bar riders coming up. Amber and the others would follow. He turned back to Ragland.

"Homer! Can you hear me?"

Ragland's eyelids fluttered again. He stared blankly at Keenlyn. "Ben?"

"Yes — it's Ben."

"Tell Emerald — I'm sorry. Tried to fix it so's she . . . we could . . . leave. What she wanted. . . . Messed it all up."

Carlin and the others pounded up and halted. The big rider's voice broke harshly through Ragland's faltering words.

"Just stand easy you two. Jack'll be here in a minute."

Keenlyn whirled angrily on him. "Shut up and get down off that horse," he snarled. "Want you to hear this."

Carlin's jaw tightened, but he dismounted and moved in close. He looked down at the rancher. "Homer Ragland," he muttered. "We figured it was one of your bunch."

Ben had turned again to the rancher. "Homer — you tried to ambush me twice. Why?"

Ragland's answer was an effort "Had to . . . get you out of . . . the way . . . sell my place. . . . Emerald said she'd leave me . . . if I . . . didn't."

Keenlyn paused, glanced at Carlin, then said, "Was it you who shot Pete?"

"There was a long space of time, the hush broken only by the dying man's labored breathing and the sound of more riders approaching.

"Was . . . me."

Carlin drew back, swearing deeply. "And us sure it was you all the time," he said to Ben.

"Why, Homer?"

"Was the only way. . . . You said . . . you'd kill him. Figured if I did you'd . . . get blamed . . . hurry things up . . . for Emerald."

"Keenlyn!" Jack Amber's voice cracked through the quiet.

Ben, on his knees, twisted around and raised his hand "Listen, Jack, Homer —"

"Hell with listening!" Amber shouted, eyes flaming with hate and anger. "I'm winding this up now!"

"Wait — Jack!" Gabe Carlin yelled. "Don't —"

Amber's gun blasted. A wave of shock smashed into Keenlyn's body and knocked him sprawling across Homer Ragland. Stunned, fury matching the pain that rocked him, Ben clawed for his pistol and fired from the hip.

Amber jolted, clutched at his chest. The weapon in his hand exploded a second shot, the effort purely reflex. The bullet dug into the ground under his horse. Slowly, stiffly, he began to topple. Gabe Carlin rushed forward, caught him, and lowered him gently.

"The fool," he muttered. "The crazy goddamn fool. If he'd only listened for once — waited."

Keenlyn, his entire left side numb, pulled himself to a sitting position and clapped his hand to the freely bleeding wound high on his shoulder. Instantly Aaron Cash, jarred from his state of frozen immobility, moved up and helped him to his feet.

Carlin straightened and faced Ben. "Reckon all I can say is I'm sorry."

"Bit late for that," Keenlyn said coldly.

Carlin shrugged. "Worked for Seven Bar. We done what Pete and Jack told us to. . . . No hard feelings?"

It seemed too easy, too simple just to call it quits. Casimiro Valdez was dead and Buck Grimmer and Chet Buntin. The Box K was ashes, cattle had been slaughtered. But there were other dead too — Pete Amber, Ragland, and now Jack. Keenlyn looked to the east, to the brilliant flare that heralded the rising sun. . . . Let it end — let the war die also.

"No hard feelings," he said, holding the folded rag Aaron handed him to his wound. "One thing you can do — get this straightened out."

"Name it."

"Ride in to town, tell the marshal and everybody else you run into. I'm tired of dodging lead."

"See to it myself," the Seven Bar ramrod said. He turned to the men lined up silently behind him. "Some of you take Jack's body to the ranch."

Keenlyn leaned heavily against Aaron Cash. A weakness was claiming his legs, and he felt the need to rest. He brushed it off impatiently, his mind still crowded, even dazed by the swift conclusion of events.

It was hard to believe that Homer Ragland was the killer. He'd given him no thought at all other than in a passing reference. It was easy to see now. Pushed to the point of desperation by Emerald, he'd been willing to do anything.

"What happens now?" Aaron asked, watching the Seven Bar riders move off. "You got to get that there wing of yours fixed and there's no ranch to head for."

Ben nodded. "Ragland's. We'll go there. Marcie's got to be told and so has Homer's wife. . . . We'll load him on my horse."

XXI

Within the week Emerald Ragland boarded the stage in Ute Springs for Kansas City, Marcie agreeing to send her a sum of money each month for living expenses. It would not afford her the life of luxury she had craved, but it would provide for her amply, and there'd never be a need for her to return to the bawdyhouse where Homer had found her.

Not long after that George Rusk quit his job and departed. No one knew why or what his destination might be. Ben Keenlyn, however, had his own ideas on the subject, but being the sort of man he was, he made no mention of it, not even to Marcie.

"Leaves Arrowhead without a foreman — and you've no ranch," she said to Ben that same evening as they sat in the cool shadows behind the house. "Can't see why we should hold off any longer. We need each other more than ever now."

He nodded. "Aim to rebuild my place someday."

Marcie looked at him closely. "We could join the ranches — combine, have a really big spread. And somewhere in the middle put up a new house."

Keenlyn grinned. "Now, that's a right good idea. . . . But this is a fine house."

"It was," Marcie said, her voice falling, "but there's no happiness left in it now. Only memories — bitter ones."

"Then a new one it'll be," he said. "I'll get things started tomorrow. We'll ride down, pick us out a good spot —"

"Not until we take care of something else first," Marcie broke in firmly.

He frowned, stared at her. "What's that? Everything's been cleared up. Hensley's gone back to Denver, there's no trouble. . . ." He paused, grinning as she pointed meaningfully at her ringless finger.

"Oh, sure — little matter of getting married. All right, get your hat. We'll go to town, roust out the preacher tonight. That soon enough?"

"Soon enough," Marcie said with a wide smile.